The Exiles
at Home

HILARY McKAY

*Hodder
Children's
Books*

A DIVISION OF HACHETTE CHILDREN'S BOOKS

To my mother

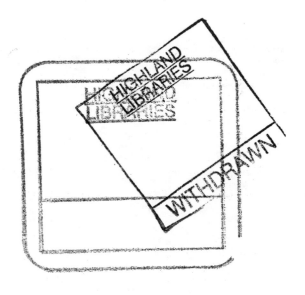

Chapter One

The Christmas holidays began with the bringing home of school reports by the four Conroy girls, and although the reports had been handed out in sealed envelopes with strict instructions from their teachers to deliver them to their parents unopened, only Phoebe's arrived home in this condition. Phoebe, who at six and three-quarters was the youngest of the Conroy girls, was so serenely detached from other people's opinions of herself and her behaviour that the report on her term's work held no temptation at all. When her mother informed her that the class teacher had written: 'Phoebe continues stubbornly to ignore all help and advice . . .' Phoebe glanced briefly up from the letter she was writing and remarked, "She always says that," before continuing unruffled with her correspondence to Father Christmas. For several weeks now, a great deal of Phoebe's time had been spent engrossed in additions and amendments to the original letter that she had written in November.

"You should post them up the chimney," Rachel told her, as Phoebe began to add the customary ingratiating row of kisses across the bottom of the page, but Phoebe preferred to leave her letters lying about where they could be discovered by her relations.

"What about your report, Rachel?" asked Mrs Conroy.

Rachel, two years older than Phoebe but far less self-assured, fumbled in her mitten for a while and then handed her mother a very wet handful of grey paper. She had (not entirely by accident) dropped her envelope in a puddle on the way home from school, in the hope of unsticking it.

It had not only unstuck, it had disintegrated, the ink had run, and during its journey home squashed in the end of Rachel's mitten, it had fallen to pieces. All that it was possible to read were the two words, 'Rachel tries . . .' Rachel brightened up tremendously at these words, so much more encouraging than she had dared to hope.

"It could be short for 'Rachel tries but fails'," her sister Naomi pointed out.

"Yes," agreed Ruth, "or 'Rachel tries to do nothing,' or 'Rachel tries to drive me mad'!"

"You're just jealous," said Rachel, "because I've got a good report and you haven't."

"No one ever gets good reports at our school," replied Ruth, who was thirteen years old and attended the local comprehensive school with twelve-year-old Naomi.

"Mine was one of the best in the class, actually. We all opened them and looked."

"Yours is disgraceful," said her mother and read aloud, "'Ruth suffers from complete lack of forethought and appears to spend a great deal of time in a daze!'"

"What's wrong with being in a daze?" asked Ruth. "Anyway, it's better than Naomi's. Hers doesn't even make sense!"

Naomi's report had puzzled everyone. It said that Naomi was one of the worst-motivated boys in the class and made no real attempt at any subject except football. Mrs Conroy read it again and passed it to Big Grandma, who had arrived that day to spend Christmas with the family.

"Frightful handwriting," commented Big Grandma cheerfully, glancing over Naomi's report, "bad example I'd have thought! Still, you must remember that it was probably written at dead of night by an exhausted, under-paid teacher, almost certainly driven mad by lack of sleep . . ."

"I wonder if I ought to complain," said Mrs Conroy.

Big Grandma, who was unsentimental, ruthless, generous and never concerned herself with details, asked, "Why persecute the poor creature?" and Mr Conroy, who had listened in silence to his daughters' reports, agreed (much to Naomi's relief).

"Christmas is no time for complaining," he said, winking at Naomi. "After all, Christmas is Christmas! Not there, Rachel!"

He was too late. Rachel, gathering together the scraps of her report, had wandered across the room searching for the magic words 'Rachel tries', and, having found them, had sat down to gloat. She sat on the Christmas cake, newly-iced and left to dry on the coffee table. Father Christmas, twelve reindeer, the North Pole and Rachel all sank together into a sudden valley of marzipan.

"I'm not eating that now!" remarked Phoebe, as Rachel ran wailing across the room, shedding tears and lumps of icing. A huge clean-up operation followed, during which Mrs Conroy forgot all about school reports. Ruth and Naomi took the cake away and resourcefully re-iced it, beautifully hilly. Father Christmas and the reindeer reappeared on cardboard skis. They sailed down the hillside beside a blue icing stream with chocolate button boulders.

"Reminds me of home," said Big Grandma when she saw it. Home for Big Grandma was Cumbria, hills and streams and sheep. The girls had spent the previous summer there and Phoebe, remembering the sheep, rinsed three plastic lambs from her farmyard and stuck them into the snow.

"Phoebe! They look grey!" exclaimed her mother.

"Sheep do look grey against the snow," said Big Grandma. "We have lambs in the village already, twins. And snow on the tops of the hills."

Naomi, thinking of the six weeks of summer spent in the Cumbrian hills, felt suddenly homesick for them. Climbing on to the window-sill she drew the curtains behind her, shutting out the bright, noisy room. The garden was grey and full of deep shadows.

'Snow!' begged Naomi silently to the dark sky, and leaning her forehead against the cold window-pane, she peered hopefully into the garden.

Ruth slid round the curtains, guessed immediately what Naomi was wishing for, and asked, "Do you think it might?"

"It's all I really want for Christmas," Naomi replied. "I don't know why it never does. It always snows in books!"

"Look! There's Broken Beak," said Ruth, as the tame family blackbird hopped out from under the hedge.

"He should be in bed. A cat might get him."

Broken Beak looked enquiringly at the house and then up at the sky.

"He's waiting for something," said Ruth.

Ruth and Naomi gazed at the dark bundle of feathers, motionless upon the lawn. Magically, as they watched, a white star appeared on his black velvet back, and then slowly, in ones and twos, more snowflakes drifted down to balance on the blades of grass. Broken Beak gave a satisfied flounce of his feathers and disappeared back under the hedge.

"It's settling!" exclaimed Naomi in delight. "Do you think Mum's forgotten about my report?"

"Ages ago. Why? Are you glad your teacher mixed them up? Do you think it would have been awful?"

"I think," said Naomi cautiously, "that Mum might not have understood what the teacher was trying to say. You know, they always have to write uncomplimentary things in case we get big-headed, but they never mean them. So they never *could* write what Mum wants to read, things like: 'Naomi has worked very hard and done extremely well and is always polite and helpful'."

"No, they'd never write that," agreed Ruth, "because it simply isn't true! They . . ."

"Anyway," Naomi interrupted hurriedly, "the snow's sticking! That's all that really matters!"

All night it snowed in their dreams. In the morning the bedroom ceilings were luminous with snow-light. It was as if they had awoken in the world of their sleep. Naomi and Ruth, who were sleeping on camp-beds in the living room so that Big Grandma could have their bedroom, rolled out at dawn to look into the garden and saw Phoebe, in her pyjamas and dressing-gown and slippers, marching solemnly across the lawn, admiring every footprint. Rachel, in pyjamas and dressing-gown but no slippers was following her, stepping carefully into her sister's footsteps so as not to spoil the snow. In places it came up to their knees.

Ruth and Naomi watched as their little sisters bent and scooped handfuls of snow into snowballs and then stowed the snowballs in their dressing-gown pockets.

"Hmm," said Ruth thoughtfully, and slid her bed across the room to barricade the door.

"Just for ten minutes," she said, "until the snowballs melt or someone catches them."

They waited until they heard footsteps in the hall and saw the door handle turning slowly. After that, there was much heavy breathing and pushing on the door, whispered orders (from Phoebe) and then retreating footsteps and the sound of the refrigerator being opened.

At breakfast time (which was late, with no bacon because of floods in the fridge) Rachel suddenly announced, "All I want for Christmas is a sledge!"

It was the first time she had been able to think of a present, although for weeks her relations had been asking, "Isn't there anything you really want, Rachel?"

"Oh yes," Rachel had replied, "a real farm and a boat. Cows and sheep and horses and donkeys. One of those hot-air balloons!" She had never thought of anything reasonable; until now, on Christmas Eve, with the roads deep in snow and more to come by the look of the sky, Rachel said, "All I want is a sledge!"

"Sorry, Rachel," said her mother, "no shopping on Christmas Eve. Not that I can think of anywhere we could find one."

"What about Father Christmas?" Rachel asked.

"Father Christmas," said Phoebe, "isn't true. Everyone knows."

"I should not care to say that," Big Grandma remarked as she consumed kippers without taking out the bones. "Certainly tempting Fate, on the twenty-fourth of December, to make rash remarks about the validity of Father Christmas!"

"Reckless," agreed Mr Conroy solemnly.

"At school," argued Phoebe, "everyone knows it's just made up for children. And Rachel's older than me! She's nearly nine!"

"And you are not yet seven and I am seventy-one," remarked Big Grandma, "so who is right?"

"I only said what they say at school. Not what I think."

"What do you think?" asked Mr Conroy.

"Thousands of things," replied Phoebe.

That day the snow muffled all sounds. It slowed the speed of cars and walkers so that their movements were soft and heavy, like movements in a dream. It drew, with its whiteness, a clean blank page over the usual scribble of their lives.

"Everything seems more real than usual," Phoebe said suddenly, as if the snow world came closer to the individual sphere on which she reposed.

Martin-next-door collected the girls to build a fort and dig paths, and Martin's dog, huge golden Josh, chased snowballs down the street and snapped at falling snow-flakes. Ruth waited until he was not looking and then buried herself in the drift under the beech hedge but Josh, in seconds, sniffed her out and snuffled and pawed the snow away.

"Josh, I love you," said Ruth as his hairy, anxious face peered down at her.

"Josh is my favourite person," remarked Rachel.

Martin, who was often called Martin-the-good, felt sud-denly Christmassy and said, "You can share him if you like. You can come round and borrow him."

"Forever, or just for the snow?" asked Rachel, believing more and more in Christmas magic.

Christmas morning came, and Rachel got her sledge.

"Where did it come from?" asked Phoebe, as Rachel stripped the wrappings away.

"Father Christmas," said Rachel, stroking and admiring her present.

"You see!" said her father.

Naomi heard Big Grandma ask her mother the same question and the whispered reply: "All yesterday after-noon with the wood he bought for the new gate. Out in the shed! I thought he'd freeze!"

Phoebe, who had kept a copy of the list of requests that she had addressed to Father Christmas, sat under the Christmas tree methodically unwrapping and ticking things off. Rachel loaded her sledge with all her unopened presents and started tugging it across the room.

"Oi! You're running me over!" said Ruth.

"Aren't you going to see what they are?" asked Mrs Conroy.

"Oh yes," said Rachel, and sitting down on her sledge, unwrapped them all saying, "Oh yes books, oh yes socks, oh yes a new bear . . ."

"He's got a zip in his back for pyjamas."

"Oh yes," said Rachel, not bothering to look. "Oh yes, chocolates!"

"Look in the envelope!"

"Oh yes, money as well! Jumpers. Pencils . . ."

"With your name on!"

"Oh yes," said Rachel and dumped all her presents back on her sledge and started pulling it across the room again.

After unwrapping a few books and some chocolates from Big Grandma (with a ten pound note each) Ruth and Naomi gloomily watched Rachel and Phoebe as they gradually submerged in an ocean of wrapping paper, until Phoebe, glancing out of the window, exclaimed, "Someone's been mucking up our snow!" and they rushed outside and followed huge black footprints to the garden shed and found two new bikes labelled 'Ruth' and 'Naomi'.

"Don't think we've ever had a better turkey," Mr Conroy innocently remarked at dinner-time.

"Free range," said Big Grandma. "Makes all the difference!"

"What do you mean?" asked Rachel.

"They wander round free," explained Mrs Conroy, "they lead more natural lives!"

Phoebe, who had eaten an enormous dinner, despite having consumed chocolates all morning, stared in horror at the turkey.

"That turkey," she announced, "is dead!"

"Certainly is," agreed Naomi cheerfully.

"Dead!" repeated Phoebe. "And that's its corpse!"

"Phoebe, really!" said Big Grandma, but Phoebe could not be stopped.

"Corpse!" she continued. "I've eaten dead corpse!" and she rushed off to the bathroom. When she emerged, pale and shaking, she announced, "I'm a vegetarian!"

★　　★　　★

The snow stayed until almost the end of the holidays, prolonging the atmosphere of Christmas. With each fresh day of sunlight and snow showers and each night of frost and stars, the feeling of other-worldness increased.

"This is the best Christmas ever," declared Rachel, who had been out from dawn to dusk, pulling a cargo of snow-balls up and down the street. "How long do you think the snow will last?"

"We've had snow in May before now," said Mr Conroy.

"Heaven forbid!" exclaimed Big Grandma. "I'm driving to Cumbria tomorrow! Anyway, the temperature's been rising all day and the weather forecast said rain for tonight."

The weather forecast proved to be correct. By morning the snow had gone, washed away by a combination of rain and Rachel's tears. Big Grandma recruited her grand-daughters to help with her packing.

"Stay a bit longer," Ruth urged. "Stay till spring!"

"Your poor mother, if I did," replied Big Grandma. "Come and sit on this suitcase lid!"

"She likes having you! We all do."

"Bounce!" ordered Big Grandma. "That's right. Now the other side. Where's Naomi?"

"She's checking that your oil and tyres and lights are all right."

"Does she know how? Perhaps we'd better go down and supervise. Just put your finger on this knot while I tie it, Ruth, and then you can carry that, and that, and that, and those, and hook a finger round this little bag and check under the bed before you come."

"Do you have to go?" Naomi, very oily and wind-swept, met Big Grandma in the hall. "Martin says the oil's all right, and three of your tyres and one of your lights."

"Which one?"

"The outside one."

"Good enough for me," said Big Grandma cheerfully,

"I'll be home before dark. Cheer up, Naomi! You can have your bed back! No more squirming on a camp-bed, being moulted on by the Christmas tree! Not that your bed is a great deal more comfortable; it's got a terrible list!"

"You could sleep in Ruth's for a change," suggested Naomi.

"It's got loose legs," said Ruth, staggering up to them under a load of Big Grandma's possessions, "but you can have it if you like. The legs only come off if you turn over quickly."

"No thank you," said Big Grandma. "At my age such novelties lose all their charm! It seems very quiet this morning. Where are Rachel and Phoebe?"

Rachel was lying on the back seat of Big Grandma's car, being dismal. "Everything nice is ending," she complained to Phoebe. "First it was end of term, then end of the day before Christmas, then end of Christmas, then end of Boxing Day, then end of the turkey, then end of last year, then end of the Christmas cake. And now it's the end of the snow and Big Grandma! That's the worst! Tonight it will be the end of the holidays!" She frowned at her feet, resting on the inside roof of the car among a pattern of small black footprints. "Look, my trainers are all worn out! Nobody cares!"

"I wish I had the keys," said Phoebe, ignoring her. "Naomi never checked the horn. I'll be legal to drive in only ten years," and she pushed in the clutch and put the car in gear. "First, second, third, fourth, reverse. All I need are the keys!"

"Big Grandma says you're to help pack!" Naomi arrived and dumped a cardboard box full of books on Rachel's stomach. "So you can open the car door when you see me coming with more stuff."

"Get that box off me, then," said Rachel.

"Ask Phoebe to," said Naomi, and dashed back through the gusty rain into the house.

"It's going to be jolly hard getting a lawn-mower in," Ruth said to Big Grandma. "Shall I take the tinsel off?"

"Certainly not! Your father must have spent hours putting it on. Help Naomi carry it out!"

"Phoebe!" croaked Rachel from the back seat, under her box of books. "I'm suffocating! I can feel my head going black!"

"Here come Ruth and Naomi with the lawn-mower," remarked Phoebe, climbing out to open the car boot.

"I've gone black!" yelled Rachel.

"Have you got the keys?" asked Phoebe.

"Mind the tinsel," ordered Naomi, "she wants to keep it. Do you think the boot will close again?"

"Well, I've fainted," said Rachel. "Serves you right, you pigs! Gone black and fainted!"

"Look at your disgusting trainers!" said Naomi reprovingly. "You've piggled holes in both of them and you've paddled mud all over the roof!"

"I didn't piggle!" Rachel indignantly unfainted for a moment. "They wore! Get this box off me!"

"Phoebe will. We're busy!"

"Give me the keys and I will," Phoebe held out her hand hopefully.

"Ho, ho, ho, little girl," said Naomi, "you must be joking!"

Back in the house, Ruth was complaining to Big Grandma. "I wish I was going back with you. There's nothing to do here."

"You must think positively," said Big Grandma. "There's always something to do! You girls have too easy a life, that's your trouble! And you've got bicycles and legs and brains, you ought to be able to entertain yourselves! Ruth's complaining to me about the dullness of Lincolnshire," she explained to Naomi.

"Well, it is!" said Naomi.

"You're an unenterprising pair! Why isn't Rachel help-ing at all?"

"She says she's gone black and fainted," explained Naomi. "Lincolnshire is boring! You know it is! That's why no one ever comes here for holidays."

"I did," pointed out Big Grandma. "Those two cases to the car, Ruth."

"How do you tell broken ribs?" asked Ruth, on returning.

"Tickle," said Big Grandma. "Don't forget my well-ingtons."

Ruth and Naomi together removed the box from Rachel's stomach and tickled her broken ribs. Rachel screamed, but sat up quickly.

"Told you they weren't broken," said Naomi.

"How do you know?" demanded Rachel.

"You'd be writhing in agony by now if they were."

Rachel writhed a bit, hoping to make her sisters feel guilty, but they had all disappeared indoors. She followed them and writhed again in front of Big Grandma.

"Do you itch somewhere?" asked Big Grandma.

"It's my broken ribs," Rachel told her crossly, as they all trooped outside.

"Must be painful," said Big Grandma. "I must be off. Don't forget to say goodbye to Martin for me! Don't for-get to write, dear!" She kissed Mrs Conroy. "Don't stand out here in the rain! Look at your daughters! All soaked except Rachel and she's got broken ribs! Deep breathing, Rachel! Kill or cure!" and she hurried into her car, tooted her horn, and was gone. Damp and disconsolate, they trailed after their mother, back into the house.

"Deep breathing!" Naomi reminded Rachel, and Rachel hugged her broken ribs and breathed deeply.

"I don't feel like going back to the ordinary world," grumbled Ruth.

"What ordinary world?" asked Phoebe.

"School and not being able to do what you like."

"I do what I like," said Phoebe.

"Yes, and look what happens to you!"

"Nothing worse than what happens to you by not doing it," pointed out Phoebe.

"S'pose not," agreed Ruth.

The next morning school began and the Conroy house filled with chaos.

"There's no time to think properly," said Naomi. "It comes too fast; it always does. It was goodbye to Big Grandma, snow melts, take down Christmas tree, bed, morning, just like dropping down a hole! Pass the marmalade, Ruth! Who put the butter right under my elbow?"

At that moment there was an enormous crash and screams and tears, the sound of them shaking the whole house.

"Rachel's fallen down the loo again," remarked Naomi, as the yells became more and more deafening. "What gets butter off?"

"Tar," answered Ruth as she grated cheese for Broken Beak, "or is it butter gets tar off? I don't know. Do you think I've done enough cheese here to last him all day? What's that awful noise?"

"I told you. Rachel's fallen down the loo again," answered Naomi. "Mum's going up to her now."

"*All right, Rachel!*" they heard their mother shout. "You *won't* go down the hole!"

"Get me out! Get me out!" Rachel continued to bawl, even when she was out and dripping on the bath mat.

"Do you think she *could* go down the hole?" asked Phoebe.

"No," said Ruth.

"Oh," said Phoebe, sounding very disappointed.

Naomi scribbled a last random answer to her holiday homework. Ruth dashed out to take Broken Beak his breakfast and to shout to Martin-next-door, who was already setting out for the bus stop, "Martin! Make the bus wait!"

"Rachel, did you see the bus?" Naomi asked, as Rachel and Mrs Conroy came downstairs.

By standing on the lavatory seat and leaning carefully out of the bathroom window it was possible to see right along the road to the bus stop before theirs. Ruth and Naomi could do this quite easily, but Rachel had to stand on tiptoe.

"I fell in," answered Rachel, "before I could see anything!"

"You Big Ones shouldn't persuade her to do it," Mrs Conroy said crossly to Ruth and Naomi. "It ruins her shoes and she might hurt herself! Not to mention the bathroom floor!"

"I don't suppose she'd go down even if we flushed it accidently?" said Phoebe thoughtfully.

"I wasn't persuaded," said Rachel, "Naomi's paying me ten pence. I'm saving up."

"What for?"

"Things for my sledge," said Rachel vaguely.

"You're a disgrace," Mrs Conroy said. "You all are! And you're going to be late again! Look at the time! And none of you ready!"

"I am." Phoebe, calm and immaculate, prepared to leave. She wore Rachel's gloves and Ruth's scarf and in her school bag was Naomi's packed lunch.

Stuffing their arms into their coat sleeves, kissing their mother and dragging scarves round their necks as they ran, her sisters followed her into the street.

Meanwhile, at the bus stop, Martin stood with one foot on the kerb and the other on the bus.

"Are you getting in?" asked the driver, "or not?"

"How much longer can you wait?"

"No longer," said the driver.

Far in the distance, the girls appeared.

"Run!" shouted Martin and the driver.

"Run!" Naomi ordered Rachel and Phoebe, "and tell them we're coming."

Rachel and Phoebe skidded off down the road and charged in to Martin.

"Go without them! Go without them!" they begged the driver.

"I can't keep doing this every morning," grumbled Martin, when Ruth and Naomi finally arrived. "I did it last term! It's awful! It's a really stressful way to start the day!"

The school bus gathered speed and overtook Rachel and Phoebe as, once more at snail's pace, they plodded along the road to their primary school. They waved frantically after the bus and Ruth, Naomi and Martin waved back.

"It's every morning, nearly!" complained Martin, "and then having to wave!"

"Well, you don't have to wave," said Ruth.

"If they wave to me, I do," replied Martin.

All along the bus, people were seated in pairs, copying each other's homework. In the back seat, Egg Yolk Wendy, the Charity Monitor, sat eating Gavin's packed lunch.

"Gavin's my new boyfriend," she called along the aisle to Ruth. "I got him at the weekend!"

Gavin stared at his knees in shame. Wendy unwrapped his chocolate biscuit and bit it in half.

"Gavin, you idiot!" said Martin. "Why'd you let her?"

"I didn't really want it," mumbled Gavin, referring to his biscuit.

Ruth, sitting next to Naomi, gazed out of the window and felt happy. It was so unusual to feel carefree and light and unencumbered on such a grey January day, that she could not understand it and wondered why. They were half-way to school before she realized.

"We've forgotten our school bags," she announced, suddenly panic-stricken, "and our games kits and lunches and library books! Let me off! Let me off!" she shouted to the driver.

Naomi slumped against the window in horror. The bus screeched to a halt.

"Somebody sick?" called the driver, "If so, get out!"

"It's no good stopping," Naomi told him. "It's too late now!"

"Good Lord in heaven," said the driver. "If I have to clean this bus again! What a way to earn a living!"

'And I'd even done my homework,' Naomi thought ruefully, 'no one will ever believe me!'

Martin realized that the poor driver thought Ruth had been sick, and he kindly wobbled up to the front of the bus to explain.

Wendy, seeing that the journey was going to take longer than usual, thought she might as well eat Gavin's apple but she said, "Do you like apples, Gav?" before she bit into it.

"Not much," said Gavin, too late to say anything else.

The driver wondered about asking for a transfer.

"How on earth are we to get through the day?" Ruth asked Naomi as they arrived at school.

"Don't know," said Naomi gloomily, and then, happening to look properly at Ruth for the first time that day, demanded, "What are you wearing?"

"What do you mean?"

"Look what you're wearing!"

Ruth looked down and nearly fainted. Tucked neatly into her school skirt was her pyjama jacket. There was nothing underneath it, and no tie or jumper on top to disguise it.

"Didn't you wash this morning?" asked Naomi, slightly shocked.

"Of course I did! I must have put it back on again! Why didn't you notice before?" Ruth began to panic for the second time that morning. "Why didn't Mum? Why didn't I?"

"Mum was fishing out Rachel and we were too busy. It's a pity it's those pyjamas though! Pink with teddy bears! You couldn't have chosen worse!"

"I didn't choose them," said Ruth, gazing with dismay at her front.

"Button up your blazer and wrap your scarf round tight," advised Naomi.

"Then what?"

"Go and hide in the library all day. No one will notice, the first day back. I'll say I don't know where you are, if anyone asks. I'll say you looked ill. You do look ill!"

Naomi departed in the direction of her classroom and Ruth slunk up the stairs to the library. It was a dim, bare room and very cold. It was so cold that Ruth collected all the books on Africa and took them away to a dark corner beside the newspapers and tried to warm herself up by reading them. She spent all day there and went home shivering. Mrs Conroy looked at her very suspiciously and put her to bed.

"They've got it next door, too," she said. "Mrs Collingwood was telling me. The baby went down with it yesterday. Martin's had it so she's hoping for the best!"

"Had what?" asked Ruth.

"Doesn't mean a thing, I told her," continued Mrs Conroy, "they catch it twice, as often as not. You'll perhaps feel better when the spots come out!"

"What spots?" demanded Ruth.

"Hanging round there all Christmas, borrowing that dog is what's done it," said Mrs Conroy. "Asking for it! Try to go to sleep! I must get down; I've left cakes in the oven."

23

"Asking for what?" Ruth called after her departing mother.

"Trouble!" Mrs Conroy called back to her. "Lie down and go to sleep!"

It was Ruth's third chicken-pox day; she was white with red dots. Her mother, saying she was less trouble in bed than out, was holding her captive in her bedroom. It was very lonely and she was glad when Naomi entered.

"Mum's been going on about our bedroom being a mess," Naomi remarked. "She sent me up to look at it."

"It's only a mess in patches," said Ruth. "Bits of it are still tidy. I'm glad you came up. I wanted to ask you to do something for me."

"I'm too busy."

"You don't know what it is yet!"

"Much too busy to do anything," said Naomi firmly, "especially if I've got to clear all this up by myself!"

"It won't take any time, hardly. And this room doesn't need clearing up, there's still lots of tidy patches."

"Well, if you don't mind looking at it," said Naomi.

"I look at the ceiling most of the time," said Ruth. "It's perfectly clear!"

Naomi flopped back on her own bed to inspect the ceiling. It was an immaculate, tidy white.

"I shan't bother then," she said, relieved.

"Good."

"Mum says I'm not to upset you because of your temperature, so perhaps I'd better leave the mess anyway."

'I am upset already,' Ruth thought, and aloud she asked, "Naomi, will you get the post for me until Mum lets me get up again?"

"Why?" asked Naomi. "What have you done?"

"Only bought something. Sort-of bought. By post, but I don't want Mum or Dad to know. Couldn't you grab the postman and get anything that comes for me?"

"Funny I never noticed before," said Naomi, still gazing at the ceiling.

"Noticed what?"

"How tidy it is."

"Will you get the post for me, then? You're not listening!"

"I am. Tell me what you've bought. Is it something alive?" Naomi became suddenly suspicious. "Or something disgusting, like those bones you collected last summer? Is that why Mum and Dad can't know? When did you buy it, anyway?"

"That awful first day at school, when I hid in the library and you told people I was ill."

"You were ill. You were sick when you got home!"

"I know. I thought it was the dog biscuits, though, not chicken-pox."

"What dog biscuits?"

"I had two in my pocket, that I was saving for Josh. I ate them for lunch. It was an awful day! Freezing cold, so I got out all the books on Africa to see if reading them would warm me up. And I looked at the newspapers from last year, and in that one that Big Grandma has, there was an advertisement." Ruth watched Naomi's face out of the corner of her eye. "It said that for only ten pounds a month you can pay for someone in Africa to go to school, and they write to you and you write back to them . . ."

"I'd pay ten pounds a month not to go to school," interrupted Naomi, "and dog biscuits are full of vitamins, it says so on the packet. Anyway, Rachel eats them!"

"So I filled in the form," continued Ruth, "and sent off for one!"

"You're nuts!" said Naomi, suddenly waking up. "Anyway, what with?"

"A pen from the lost property drawer."

"I meant, what money?"

"Big Grandma's ten pounds," said Ruth, sighing. "You

have to send the first month's money and fill in a form to say you'll sponsor whoever it is for at least a year, and say that you're over eighteen."

"Well, you're not!"

"I know. I wrote a thirteen that looked like an eighteen! It's too late now! They'll send me off and say I've ordered a boy and he'll start school and he'll write to me and how can I tell him he's got to stop? I don't know," gabbled Ruth, ignoring Naomi's astonished face. "It's probably against the law and not legal, it was because of Christmas being so Christmassy and everything had been so nice here and no food there, not turkey anyway, and Big Grandma said we were unenterprising and I thought it would be nice to know someone in Africa to write to and that first day back was so awful! It must have been chicken-pox fever made me do it! What are you staring at me like that for?"

"You've bought an illegal boy in Africa?" asked Naomi, amazed. "For ten pounds a month? You can't buy people!"

"I know that, now!"

"And he's going to write to you, and you have to send off ten pounds every month? And you've started it already! You never have any money, none of us do! He's not going to think much of you, when you tell him the truth! And what about the people who organize it? You'll have to write and explain you were mad with chicken-pox and ask for your ten pounds back and they'll probably have spent it! I bet it's not that easy to get it back!"

"I know, I'm not going to, and anyway I don't think it's such a bad idea. Or it wouldn't be, if I had any money. But I can't tell Mum, you know how she hates us sending away for things and she'd be furious about me saying I was eighteen. So would Dad. They'll say it isn't honest!"

"Well, it isn't," said Naomi virtuously. "Anyway, what do you want me to do?"

"Just get the post, that's all. Until I can get up again."

"Oh, all right," agreed Naomi, "but it's all I'm doing to help!"

The African countryside outside the classroom windows was not so much coloured as shaded with light. The brightness of the day faded the colours until they drifted together. Shades of dust and shapes blown by the wind patterned the landscape. It was all the world that Joseck had ever seen.

'But not all I know,' he thought.

The little wooden school was full of echoes of other places, other languages and other lives. Joseck listened to the echoes and wondered, and it seemed to him that he was part of a world he could not see, and sometimes he thought that it did not matter and sometimes he knew that it did.

Today he knew that it did, because as a result of Ruth's happy Christmas and Big Grandma's ten pounds and the turmoil in the Conroy household in the morning and Martin-the-good's baby brother's chicken-pox, the teacher said:

"You have a sponsor this year, Joseck!"

Chapter Two

For the next few days Naomi watched the post for Ruth, hanging round the gate until the postman came and then volunteering to take the letters inside. As the days went on, an understanding grew between the postman and Naomi, that she was waiting for a letter from her boy-friend, and he would wink knowingly at her, as he handed the morning's post over Rachel and Phoebe's grabbing hands.

"Sorry old lady," he would say, when morning after morning there was nothing but bills for her parents. "He must be a hard-hearted young blighter!" Naomi smiled a suitably forlorn and love-struck smile at him.

"You're a proper little Mona Lisa," said the postman, and then spoilt it by adding, "never could see anything in that picture myself!"

Waiting for the post to come made them even later than usual for the school bus every morning. This was most unpopular. The bus driver grumbled at Martin, who daily took his heroic stance, one foot on the kerb and the other on the bus. Wendy got frightfully indignant one day and protested to Naomi that it made her late for everything. Even Gavin, the mildest of people, confided in a whisper to Martin that it gave Wendy more time than usual to eat his packed lunch. Martin passed this complaint on to Naomi, together with several of his own, and Naomi in turn reported them all to Ruth, who was still confined in their bedroom, quite poorly but recovering slowly.

"Sorry," said Ruth.

One morning the postman, grinning and humming

'Mona Lisa' as he came down the street, handed Naomi a very scruffy envelope addressed to 'R.N.R.P. Conroy'.

"Is that you?" he asked.

"Yes, thank you," replied Naomi, recognizing one of the rare, welcome letters from Graham, their friend of the summer holidays. Graham's letters, usually written at the kitchen table of the Cumbrian farm which was his home, were largely incomprehensible to the girls, but none the less treasured. They were full of descriptions of football matches, farm machinery and local weather conditions and always began, 'Mum says I ought to write . . .'

"Hope it's been worth the wait," said the postman sympathetically, but the next morning he was quite annoyed when Naomi appeared again with her hand held out.

"You can't expect the poor lad to write every day," he said severely. "There's just one for your sister," and he delivered the long-awaited brown envelope over to Naomi rather reprovingly. Naomi carried it in to Ruth between her fingertips, as if it might explode.

"I'm glad it's Saturday," she said crossly, "you can get the post yourself on Monday! It's too embarrassing!"

"Don't you want to know what it says?" asked Ruth, seeing that Naomi was preparing to leave again.

"I'm going into town," replied Naomi. "Anyway, I told you I didn't want anything to do with it, and I don't! Will Mum let you out today, do you think?"

"No she won't!" said Mrs Conroy, appearing suddenly in the doorway. "Don't stuff things under your jumper, Ruth! You'll make it go all baggy! No, Ruth isn't going anywhere today; she can have a quiet weekend before school on Monday. And Rachel and Phoebe aren't moving one step out of my sight until they've tidied up their bedroom!"

Ruth and Naomi peered curiously round their little sisters' bedroom door. Rachel and Phoebe were sitting sulkily on their bunk-beds, obviously appalled at the prospect before them. The entire bedroom floor, except for a narrow track leading to the bunks, was covered in toys, books, clothes and bits of paper.

"I can't find my Snoopy socks," said Phoebe.

"I'm surprised you can find your feet in all that mess," said Mrs Conroy crossly, "and it's about time that sledge went down to the shed, waking us up every night! I must have the only daughter in England that takes a sledge to bed with her!"

"Does she take it to bed with her?" asked Naomi, surprised. "Is that what the crashes are? I thought it was only Rachel falling out!"

"Yes," said Phoebe, "every night, and then when it falls out, she gets up and drags it back up again and treads all over my face. And what if it falls on my head, that's what I say?"

"Tie it to the bed," suggested Naomi practically.

"Then when it falls off, it swings down and whacks Phoebe. I've tried that," said Rachel.

"Crash, into the side of the bed!" Phoebe told Naomi. "And Rachel said, 'Oh, is it broken? Is it broken?' *Then* she fell out of bed."

"Well, you took away the steps in the dark!"

"Everything to be put away before I come back up!" interrupted Mrs Conroy, closing the door on their squabbles. "Or I shall do it myself and It Will All Go In The Bin!"

Ruth disappeared to lock herself in the bathroom, where she could read her letter in peace. Naomi, whose Christmas money had been weighing on her mind ever since she had received it, prepared to go up to the town.

"Don't go wasting it all at once," advised Mrs Conroy.

"I'm only going to look at things," said Naomi, smoothing and admiring her ten pound note. She had begun to dream about it at night and it was the first thing she thought of when she woke up. She had no intention of spending it, but on that lonely, grey January Saturday, she rashly took it up to town with her. And that was the end of it.

Some days later, she tried to explain to Ruth what had happened to her money. "Glue," she remembered. "I bought some glue. We never have any; ours is always all dried up."

"What glue?" asked Ruth.

"Well, it's all dried up now, too. And I bought some gold stars, like they used to stick on our books at junior school. Two packets. I took them to school."

Ruth recollected the stars but was too kind to say anything. Naomi had stuck them all over her books and subsequently spent two detentions peeling them off again.

"And one of each of all the tropical fruits in the supermarket, and some strawberries!"

"In January!"

"And a newspaper. To sit on while I ate the fruit; the bench was wet."

"What was the fruit like?"

"Some of it was awful. And a lamb chop and a packet of chocolate biscuits for a poor thin dog that was tied to a bench."

"That was nice."

"And a football magazine, to try and find out what Graham was talking about. But Martin's borrowed it; I'll get it back though, before we write to Graham. And some stamps. And some dog chocs for teaching Josh tricks with, but Rachel's been eating them."

"That must have been nearly all your money, then," said Ruth.

"Yes," said Naomi, "that was nearly all of it. It went fast."

"What a waste!"

"Well, look what you did with yours!" exclaimed

Naomi, "and you've said you'll pay ten pounds a month for at least a year and you only get a pound a week pocket money, so even if you don't spend a penny of it, you'll be minus six pounds a month!"

"I was going to let you share him," said Ruth.

"No thank you!"

"Well, you could just look at the stuff they sent." Ruth pulled her envelope out from under her mattress. "I've even got a photograph of him. He's ten and he's called Joseck."

"Joseph?" asked Naomi, peering over Ruth's shoulder at the picture of a thin, wise-eyed African boy, dressed in immaculate white and holding an armful of books.

"No, Joseck. And it says I can go and visit him one day!"

"'Course you couldn't!"

"I might do one day. Anyway, it's nice to be asked. He's got eleven brothers and sisters all older than him."

Naomi took the papers from Ruth and began reading them for herself.

"Fancy not knowing when his birthday is," she commented. "That must be weird! He looks very brainy. Says you can't send presents to him. Good job really, we haven't any money!"

"I looked up where he lives in my school atlas," said Ruth.

Naomi was still studying the photograph.

"He looks nice," she said eventually. "Pity to have to let him down. When do you need the next ten pounds for?"

"Next week," replied Ruth, and they both stared thoughtfully out of the window.

"You'll have to tell Mum and Dad," said Naomi eventually.

"I sort of mentioned it," said Ruth.

When Ruth had casually mentioned sponsoring children, Mrs Conroy had seemed to disapprove of the whole scheme. Not that she was reluctant to give money to a good cause, she said, and in fact she and Mr Conroy gave a regular amount each month, deducted straight from Mr Conroy's salary.

"I didn't know!" Ruth was surprised.

"But I don't believe in singling out individual children and expecting them to write grateful letters," concluded Mrs Conroy firmly. "I shouldn't like any of you to have to do it. All children have a right to be educated, wherever they live."

"But I wanted him for a sort of pen-friend," said Ruth, explaining all this to Naomi, "not to be grateful to me. I didn't think of that. I wanted to know someone in Africa."

"Ten pounds by next week," said Naomi thoughtfully. "We'd better go and see what Rachel and Phoebe have done with their money."

Rachel and Phoebe were out in the back garden, being taught to groom Josh, under Martin's supervision. Josh had been brushed and brushed until he shone and handfuls of his red-gold fur were floating all over the garden.

"You'll brush him bare," remarked Naomi. "He looks thinner already."

"We've cleaned his teeth," said Rachel, "with dog tooth-paste. It's peppermint, like people's!"

"Did you eat it?"

"Only a bit."

"I've always wanted a horse," said Phoebe, dreamily combing the feathers on Josh's front legs.

"Yes, but he's a dog," pointed out Martin.

"I know, but I call him a horse in my head," answered Phoebe, who could always ignore reality when she needed to.

Naomi gave Rachel and Josh one each of her remaining dog chocs. They both sat up and begged.

"It's nice for Josh not to be the only one who has to beg," said Ruth, watching them. "He must feel a fool doing it on his own."

"More likely feels a fool doing it with Rachel," answered Martin.

Phoebe took two of the dog chocs and tried to make Rachel and Josh balance them on their noses, but they both jerked their heads and ate them at once.

"Can I have two more?" asked Phoebe.

"You should buy some yourself," said Naomi, "you've got all that money that Big Grandma gave you."

"Yes, but I put it in my train," explained Phoebe, "before I thought."

Ruth and Naomi sighed with frustration. Phoebe's train, given to her by Big Grandma as a christening present, was very old and, Mrs Conroy said, quite valuable. Its enormous disadvantage was that although it had a slot to put your money in, there was no way of getting it back out again. Careful shaking sometimes allowed the reckless saver to extract coins from its insides, but paper money was gone for good. Everyone knew Phoebe was in the habit of writing important messages to herself and stuffing them in her train, but it had occurred to no one that she might push her money into it as well.

"Anyway, it's safe there," said Phoebe comfortably, "Rachel's lost hers!"

Ruth looked at Naomi in despair. Never, it seemed, could forty pounds have been disposed of with so little to show for it.

"I haven't," said Rachel, "I've put it in a secret place."

"In the house?"

"No."

"In the garden?"

"No."

"Not at school somewhere?"

"'Course not."

"Are Mum and Dad looking after it for you, then?"

"No."

"Sounds like you've lost it," said Naomi.

"Why d'you want to know?" Rachel asked suspiciously.

"I don't," said Naomi. "I was just thinking about money. I was wondering how people got it."

"They go to work and earn it," said Martin. "My dad says the only money worth having is money you've earned yourself!"

"Well, why does he do the football pools every week, then?" asked Ruth. "That's the best way of getting money, earning it's too slow. Winning is much quicker!"

"You can sell things," said Phoebe, "like I will sell you my train for a thousand pounds. Nine-hundred-and-ninety pounds profit for me!" and she held out her hand. Naomi gave her a dog choc.

"What we need," said Naomi, "are rich relations."

"You've got them," said Martin. "One, anyway. Your gran."

"I don't think she's rich," said Naomi thoughtfully. "She doesn't spend much."

"That's how you get rich," said Martin wisely.

"The best way," said Rachel, scrabbling through a flower bed as she spoke, "is to find treasure. Buried treasure. Lumps of gold and rings and diamonds. I've found something already! What is it?"

"A tulip bulb," said Ruth, taking it off her and inspecting it. "Put it back!"

"Treasure," repeated Rachel dreamily. "People do. Look how I found that bulb without even trying! Gold and diamonds and stuff, it must be all over the place! Jewellers' shops are full of it, and it's all got to come from somewhere, dug up or out of caves, I think. Everyone's got some, even Mum's got a bit. And what happens to all the old stuff? It must be lying around somewhere!"

Everyone stared at Rachel. Obviously she had given the subject a great deal of thought.

"Old stuff gets melted down, I suppose," said Martin practically.

"I've never heard of anyone melting it down!"

"Or put in museums."

"I've been to a museum," argued Rachel. "It was full of old china and old clothes and boring statues. Hardly any treasure. I looked."

At that moment a diversion was created. Mrs Collingwood, Martin's mother, appeared round the corner of the house with a push-chair. In it, screaming, sat Martin's little brother.

"Darling, I'm going to have to leave Peter with you," Mrs Collingwood announced, parking the push-chair beside Martin. "Daddy will be back soon after nine. Give him some tea and see if you can get him off to bed. Perhaps the girls will help!"

Martin's mother was a solicitor; she was clever and practical, and assumed that everyone else was as well, except those unfortunate people who demanded (from the police station) that she come and rescue them. Ruth and Naomi could never decide whether they liked her or not. She always spoke to them as if they shared something wonderful together, a joke perhaps, or a secret, a common understanding that reflected rather well on all of them. Rachel adored Martin's mother because Martin's mother always called her 'My Little Pet'. Rachel thought that Mrs Collingwood was the only person who realized how very nice Rachel really was, or could be, if it was convenient for Rachel to be nice all the time, which it wasn't. Phoebe, however, more or less detested Mrs Collingwood, because quite often she called Phoebe 'My Sausage'. Phoebe did not like to think of herself as anyone's sausage.

Now Mrs Collingwood bent down to Peter's teary, purple, dripping face and said, "Smile for your mummy!

36

Smiley-smiley! One little smile!" and as Peter's screwed-up features uncreased for a minute, she said, "That's my little treasure!" kissed him, and was gone.

"Not what I call treasure!" said Rachel scornfully. Martin's mother had hardly closed the Conroys' garden gate behind her before Peter hiccuped and took an enormous breath to start again.

Ruth gazed thoughtfully at Peter. He was not what she called treasure, either. Still a bit chicken-poxy, practically bald although he was nearly two, he was horribly uninhibited, and equipped, Martin had told her, with very sharp teeth. Usually Ruth would have kept as far away as possible, but now she had a person in Africa whom she had promised to educate, at the enormous cost of ten pounds a month. And here was Peter, crying out (literally) for a baby-sitter.

Naomi, Rachel and Phoebe had disappeared with a suddenness that was not flattering to Peter. Even Josh had jumped over the garden wall and gone home.

"Do you need some help?" Ruth asked Martin, above the din that his little brother was making.

Martin could not control Peter. He tried to reason with him, and Peter was not a reasonable person. Dimly, Ruth understood this. Peter was raw, brute creation, like Rachel and Phoebe. Perhaps she could do something with him.

"Do you need some help?" she repeated.

"What can you do?" asked Martin, not fainting with gratitude as Ruth had hoped he would. "I agree you ought to do something, considering the number of times I've held up the bus for you, but what can you do?"

"I could probably stop him screaming," said Ruth. "Me and Naomi invented a way to stop Phoebe screaming when she was little. It nearly always worked."

"Well, you're not to hurt him. Why doesn't everyone

do it if it works? Peter's been screaming for nearly two years!"

"Not everyone is strong enough to do it," replied Ruth, "or they haven't got a long, straight place to run in. We used to do it in the park. Is he strapped in tight?"

"Of course he is. He escapes otherwise."

"Good," said Ruth, wheeling Peter out of the gate and on to the path. "Now you run along on the outside, by the kerb, just in case!" and taking a deep breath, she began to push Peter along, faster and faster, until the hedges went past in a blur and the ground looked like a grey river beneath her feet and they reached the end of the road and swung back round, and Martin no longer had breath to shout "What are we doing?" and Peter, far from screaming, was roaring with laughter and slapping his fat knees. By the time they reached the garden gate again, there was not a trace of a tear on his face.

"See?" said Ruth complacently, when she got her breath back. "It used to work just like that on Phoebe, only Mum could never do it because she couldn't run fast enough."

"Good dog! Good dog!" shouted Peter, whacking the sides of his chariot.

"Now what?" asked Martin.

"Well," said Ruth, "then it's the hard bit. You have to do it again only a bit slower, and then again, and then perhaps again until you get down to walking. After that you can stop, because they're usually exhausted."

"*They're* exhausted!" interrupted Martin.

"You can push this time," Ruth told him, and at the end of the second run, Peter was distinctly drooping. "He can't be as tough as Phoebe was," remarked Ruth, surveying him. "Take him indoors and feed him quick, before he goes to sleep. You might even be able to get him to bed."

Peter glanced at Ruth. He could not tell her that he had been terribly bored and frustrated and that she had been fast and exciting and had allowed him to stop screaming, but nevertheless, he was grateful.

"Good dog," said Peter approvingly.

"That means 'thank you'," translated Martin. "Thanks."

"That's all right," said Ruth, as Peter was escorted indoors. Possibly, she thought, she would become indispensable and could put her baby-sitting prices up and up, to say, ten pounds an hour, or even more. She could get rich. Perhaps Peter was a treasure, after all. Visions of herself as a next-door, very expensive, very exclusive Mary Poppins filled her mind.

"That worked quickly," remarked Naomi as Ruth, rather pink-faced from running in the cold air, returned indoors. "Phoebe didn't believe me when I told her we used to do that to her!"

"Mum wouldn't have let you," said Phoebe, looking very mutinous.

"Mum wouldn't have let you what?" asked Mrs Conroy, opening the dining room door at that moment. "Lay the table please Ruth, and Naomi, pop and make the salad, will you? You two Little Ones, clear up all this mess!"

"Mum, you wouldn't have let them run me up and down in a push-chair to stop me screaming, would you? Anyway, I didn't scream!"

"Round and round the park they used to push you," recalled Mrs Conroy smiling, "I remember now!"

"What if I'd fallen out?" asked Phoebe, outraged.

"You were strapped in. Anyway, they didn't go all that fast. Ruth would only have been about eight. Come on, clear up all that chopped-up paper, Phoebe!"

Phoebe had been converting the box that her Christmas slippers arrived in, into a cage. Cardboard bars were glued across the front, and now she stuck a notice across the top saying,

'BEWAR OF THE'

Carefully Phoebe carried her cage to the window-sill and propped up along its bottom the rest of the sentence,

'RORIN PIG'

Between the bars she slid the latest school photograph of Ruth.

"Well really, Phoebe," exclaimed Mrs Conroy, although she could not help laughing. "It was all a long time ago!"

"I don't care," said Phoebe. "I'm starting a zoo." She fetched her bear from the bedroom and sat him outside the cage so that he could see Ruth, the Roaring Pig, in the zoo.

Tea-time was unusually quiet that day. Ruth, once again preoccupied by her urgent need for money, ignored all Phoebe's dark glances towards the zoo on the window-sill. Rachel was depressed by the thought that it was her turn to wash up after tea. Partly to postpone the awful event, she finished off all the bread and butter and took a third helping of salad.

"Can I have some of Phoebe's sardines?" she asked. "I've run out of ham."

"Is Phoebe eating sardines?" asked Naomi in surprise. "I thought she was a vegetarian!"

"I am." Phoebe, carefully shrouding a sardine in a lettuce leaf, looked up defensively.

"Sardines are animals," argued Naomi.

"Leave Phoebe alone," Mr Conroy interrupted. "If she's happy eating sardines, let her enjoy them in peace!"

"They haven't got legs," said Phoebe, but all the same she unwrapped her sardine and gazed at it uncertainly. Across the table Rachel watched her, hoping.

"They've got tails," she remarked.

40

"Enough of this conversation," announced Mrs Conroy firmly. "Rachel, you can start clearing the table. Ruth and Naomi will help you. Phoebe, finish your tea properly!"

"I can't," said Phoebe, "they *have* got tails!"

"Then you must eat some cheese instead!"

Phoebe sat mutinously at the table with her father, while Mrs Conroy left to supervise the washing-up.

"Pass me your plate," said Mr Conroy, "and I'll make you a sandwich."

Phoebe passed over her plate and her father reassembled its contents into a more discreet form. "There you are," he said, "what the eye doesn't see . . . Why have you stuck poor old Ruth in prison?"

"It's a zoo, not a prison."

"Just as bad."

"It was a case of offended dignity," said Mrs Conroy, reappearing for a moment.

Phoebe, chewing her sandwich, left the table to poke a bit of lettuce through the bars to Ruth.

"What if I took her out?" asked Mr Conroy.

"She would still be in," replied Phoebe, "in my mind."

"What did she do?"

"Said I screamed," explained Phoebe with her mouth full, "when I was a baby. Like Peter next door. I didn't, did I?"

"Never," said Mr Conroy solemnly, "you were the soul of discretion."

"Did Ruth and Naomi scream?"

"Continually," Mr Conroy told her.

Phoebe looked pleased and, swallowing the last of her sandwich, leaned companionably against her father as she admired her captive.

"You wouldn't put your poor old dad in a zoo for offending your dignity, would you?" asked Mr Conroy, looking down at her.

"No," said Phoebe.

41

In the kitchen, Rachel dumped piles of plates into the washing-up bowl and pulled them out again in handfuls.

"I'm not drying that," said Naomi, "it's still got a whole sardine on it."

"I'll wash if you like," Ruth offered, "for twenty pence."

"Ten," said Rachel.

"All right."

"D'you need money that much?" asked Naomi, as Rachel vanished before Ruth could change her mind.

"You know I do. I'm going to see if I can baby-sit for Peter, but I still need ten pounds now. I've got to send it off. I've only got three pounds' pocket money saved up. How much have you got?"

"Three," said Naomi before she thought, "and a bit of change from Big Grandma's money, about eighty pence."

"That's six pounds-eighty then," said Ruth. "Six pounds-ninety with Rachel's money."

"Well, I want mine back," said Naomi. "You can have it for now, as a loan, but it's February next month. Mum and Rachel and Phoebe's birthdays."

Beside the kitchen sink stood an old wooden Dutch clog, into which the Conroys were in the habit of dropping all the odds and ends found lying round the kitchen. Ruth emptied its contents on to the kitchen table. There were several buttons and elastic bands, two biro tops and the three plastic lambs that had been on the Christmas cake, a scattering of coppers and a few five pence pieces, a tooth, half a packet of mustard and cress seed, and a diamond and sapphire ring.

"Good heavens!" said Mrs Conroy, coming in and picking it up. "Mother's engagement ring! I didn't even know she'd lost it!"

"Can I have the change?" asked Ruth, "for charity?"

"Yes, I suppose so," agreed Mrs Conroy, turning over the contents of the clog. "Rachel's tooth! I never know what to do with teeth! It seems a bit heartless to throw them away. Some mothers keep them, and first shoes and bits of hair and goodness knows what."

"So what do you do with them?" asked Naomi.

"Well, throw them away, I'm afraid," confessed Mrs Conroy. "After all, there's four of you, it would end up as bad as Ruth's bone collection if I didn't. And I once caught Rachel recycling teeth, taking them off my dressing table and putting them back under her pillow. Your father paid out night after night without noticing! Thank you for washing up!"

"If we find any more bits of money lying about, can we keep it?" asked Naomi. "It's for charity."

"If you're that hard-up," agreed Mrs Conroy, "one good turn deserves another! Something's been rattling round the washing machine, if you want to unscrew the filter and have a look. And there's twenty pence in your father's shaving mug, and speaking of good turns, I've been meaning to mention. I'm going back to work this spring. You two Big Ones especially, are going to find yourselves helping out a bit more."

"Back to nursing?" asked Ruth. "Can you remember how?"

"There's a refresher course," Mrs Conroy said, "it will only be part-time, evenings perhaps, or mornings. Bank nursing, they call it; they bring you in when they need extra staff. It's about time I got back to work again!"

Ruth, grovelling round the back of the washing machine, emerged with forty pence and a lot of fluff.

"Shall you mind going back?"

"I knew," said Naomi unexpectedly. "Big Grandma told me. She said we'd have to help with Rachel and Phoebe while you were out, till Dad came home. Well, at least they're house-trained, not like Peter! There's thirty-two pence in this shoe," and she pushed the change over to Ruth.

"I hope it's for a good cause," remarked Mrs Conroy, watching them. "Yes, I always enjoyed nursing, and Grandma tells me you managed very well last summer, looking after yourselves a bit."

"Did she?" asked Naomi, looking very surprised.

"You're growing up fast now," continued Mrs Conroy, ignoring Naomi on purpose. "Time you had a bit more responsibility."

Ruth and Naomi wondered what their mother would say if she knew how much responsibility they had recently undertaken. It did not seem quite the time to tell her, however, so they merely smiled and said they would help.

"Six pounds-ninety, seven pounds-thirty, seven pounds sixty-two," counted Ruth when Mrs Conroy had gone. "Fancy Mum starting work again, seven pounds-eighty-two," she added, when Naomi produced the shaving mug's twenty pence, "I can't imagine it somehow."

"We ought to try scooping down the backs of the living room chairs," suggested Naomi. "We haven't done it for ages, Big Grandma said it would be good for all of us."

"Scooping down chairs?"

"Mum going to work."

"Oh."

The chairs produced a further fifty-eight pence, six combs, numerous hair-slides and a quantity of nutshells.

"Eight pounds-forty," said Naomi, "and that's the lot. We won't be able to do this again you know, all this must have been piling up for ages."

Despite further searching, that really did seem to be the lot, and it had taken all evening to find. Peter unexpectedly saved the situation in the morning.

"Darling!" Mrs Collingwood stopped Naomi as she passed the house. "My poor Peter owes you an apology, I'm afraid! Dreadfully sick all over your mag last night!" And she showed Naomi the damp and disgusting remains of her football magazine. Naomi stepped backwards hastily.

"Hopeless," agreed Mrs Collingwood. "Washed it, but hopeless. You'll have to get yourself another! Can't say I'm sorry, because it might have been the carpet. Usually is, to be frank; anyway, Martin says two pounds will cover it, so there we are, and we're very sorry, aren't we Peter-pet?"

Peter, who was squirming in his mother's arms, did not look sorry. He hung his tongue out at Naomi, and then grabbed the magazine off his mother and stuffed it in his mouth.

"Chews everything!" remarked Mrs Collingwood cheerfully. "Poor darling, no discretion! Wave bye-bye!"

Naomi, not quite sure who was being addressed, herself or Peter, waved bye-bye.

"Good old Peter," said Ruth, pale with relief when she heard the news. "He *is* a treasure! In a way!"

"'Good old Naomi', you should say," commented Naomi, "I could have kept the money, it was my magazine!"

"I know."

"This is the Last Time," said Naomi firmly. "The Last Time I help!"

Chapter Three

It was in January that the teacher said to Joseck, "You have a sponsor this year, Joseck!"

Joseck had had a sponsor for three years already. Then there had been notification to say that the sponsor had stopped.

"Why?" asked Joseck. "I wrote the letters."

The letters were written all together in class. In the past, not many of the children had been sponsored, but this year the school had been lucky, nearly everyone had someone, somewhere, to write to. On the blackboard the teacher wrote guide-lines for the children to follow:

> About your family and home
> About your school work
> About yourself

English was a second language to the children, and some, especially the younger ones, struggled hard to compose these letters to strangers in unknown lands.

One small girl said, "No."

"No what?"

She stared out of the window; nose in the air, chin in her hands, completely stubborn, she might have been Phoebe in a different life.

"I won't write. I won't say thank you."

"You don't have to say thank you," said the teacher, "but write something. Write your name."

"I am Mari," wrote Mari. The page still looked very empty.

"You might draw a picture," the teacher suggested gently. "Draw a picture of yourself."

Mari drew a picture. It was not very good; for a start it was blue, because that was the colour of the airmail letter.

"Is that like you, do you think?" asked the teacher.

"I am not blue," said Mari, golden in the African sunlight streaming through the window, "and I am much more beautiful."

That was true.

Joseck loved to write the letters, and to receive the postcards and pictures that came back in return; nearly every month there were some for the teacher to hand out, although hardly ever any for Joseck himself.

"Some sponsors write more than others," explained the teacher, and, "Sorry Joseck," he would say when there were no letters for him, but now today he said, "You have a new sponsor, Joseck!"

Joseck jumped.

"You will have to write the letters again," said Mari to him, "blue letters," she added darkly.

"I like writing letters," said Joseck. "Can we write today?"

"Today," agreed the teacher, and Joseck wrote,

> Dear Sponsor,
>   I am happy to write again this term. How is everything in your country? I hope you have no problem in your area.
> I am well. I am going on well with my studies. My favourite is maths and football. Many books are waiting for me to read. And so I will stop writing.

Joseck paused. There was a question he wanted to ask, but he thought it was not quite polite.

I should like to know, he wrote,
why you are my sponsor?

"Is that all right?" he asked the teacher.
"Yes, I think so," said the teacher.
Your loving child Joseck, signed Joseck.

Even in ordinary years, February was a month that stretched the girls' resources to their limits.

"Three birthdays *and* a boy to educate!" said Naomi, sighing.

"I'm not bothering with Phoebe's birthday unless she takes me out of the zoo," Ruth replied.

"Neither will I, then," agreed Naomi.

"Neither will you what?" asked Rachel.

"Bother with Phoebe's birthday unless she takes us out of the zoo."

"I won't either then," said Rachel.

"Are you in there, too?"

"I got put in yesterday. She made another cage, just for me. You go and look, it's awful."

Sure enough, there were now three cages lined up on the living room window-sill. Ruth and Naomi glared through the bars of one, on which the notice had been changed to 'Rorin PigS', another contained cardboard effigies of Phoebe's teacher and the Lollipop Lady (recognizable by her Lollipop). 'Not Tame Yet' read their description. In the third, on a bit of straw, languished Rachel alone, unkindly labelled, 'The Slege Monster'.

"See?" said Rachel.

"What did you do?"

"Nothing, she just hates my sledge, that's all."

"Did it fall on her in the night again?"

Rachel did not answer, but rattled the bars of her cage rather moodily.

48

"Well, you don't have to do anything," said Naomi, "I didn't. I just got put in for no reason at all."

"You were ROBBING MY TRAIN!" said a voice through a crack in the door. "I caught you at it!"

Phoebe appeared, clutching her train and a tin-opener. "With a knitting needle! You know you were!"

"I was only seeing if anything would come out."

"Did anything?"

"No."

"Lucky for you," said Phoebe ominously.

"I'd have given it to you if it had."

"I came to see if you wanted any ideas for my birthday," said Phoebe, "because I've thought of something I . . ."

"We're not bothering about your birthday unless you let us out of the zoo," interrupted Ruth.

Phoebe said nothing, but continued to fish down the slot of her train with the bottle-opener bit of the tin-opener. Tiny bits of paper came up on the hook.

"You'll chop that ten pound note to pieces if you're not careful," warned Naomi.

Phoebe ignored her.

"You're probably squashing it further and further in. Let me have a go."

Phoebe handed her train over to Ruth, who poked and poked and achieved nothing.

"What about the vacuum cleaner?" suggested Naomi. "It might suck it out."

It did not suck it out; they wasted an hour on it before they gave up, at the end of which Phoebe evidently felt more kindly towards her sisters. She did not let them out, but she fed them bits of biscuit through the bars and made them cotton wool nests. Martin came round while they were admiring them, took one look, and said rashly that Phoebe obviously had a personality problem. Phoebe tore out of the room to look for a box.

"Now she's gone," said Martin to Ruth, "will you come

49

round and look at Peter and tell me if Phoebe did anything like he's doing now?"

It did not sound a very tempting invitation, but it was another opportunity to make herself indispensable to Peter, and so Ruth agreed.

"Did she do that?" asked Martin, ushering Ruth into the Collingwoods' large and gleaming kitchen.

"Oh yes," said Ruth, looking in at Peter. "That sort of thing, anyway."

Peter, strapped in his high chair, was covered in butter and crumbs, beating his fists as hard as he could on his blue plastic table. Under the fists were crumbs that had been crisps, and all over the floor around Peter were more crumbs and lumps of sandwich, a feeding cup, evidently hurled there, his bunny rabbit plate, his shoes and his socks.

"His tea is all ready," said Martin, indicating the stack of miniature egg sandwiches, the crisps and the cubes of cheese, so far untouched on the dresser. "Mum said to give it to him, because you can't keep him waiting once he's seen it and she had to dash out."

"Does she always get so much ready?" asked Ruth. It looked an awful lot for a two-year-old, and Peter had evidently demolished quite a lot already.

"Oh no," said Martin, "only when she knows I'll have to feed him. It takes such a lot to get any in."

"Can't Josh come and eat up the bits on the floor?"

"He's not allowed. He'll get too fat and it just makes Peter throw down more scraps for him."

"What does he do when you give him a sandwich?"

"I'll show you."

Peter grabbed the sandwich, ripped it in half, squeezed it through his fists, chewed his knuckles, flung one handful on to the carpet, hammered the rest flat on his tray, licked up the remains, and turned and dribbled them over the edge.

"Does he do that with your mother?"

"Oh no," said Martin, "but did Phoebe do that?"

"Well, sometimes. Don't tell her I said so, though."

"What did you do?"

"Mum used to say, 'Right then, we'll fetch Rachel!'"

"What did Rachel do?"

"Well, she ate everything."

"Even the screwed-up bits?"

"Oh yes, usually."

Martin looked at Peter's screwed-up bits and shuddered. "I'm not."

"No, but it's the right idea. We should take everything away, and tidy up, just as if he'd had it."

Peter watched in horror as they cleaned the floor, wiped down his chair, washed his hands and arms and elbows and face and head ("Good job he hasn't much hair," commented Ruth) and removed the food from sight. He opened his mouth and howled.

"Very nice sandwiches," said Ruth, taking one out of the fridge and eating it. "Have one too."

Martin obediently took one, and Peter watched in disbelief as his private slave consumed his tea. Ruth, taking another one, cut it in half and eating one bit herself, put the other on Peter's tray. Peter made a grab for it, but Ruth got there first.

"That's what Rachel used to do to Phoebe." She put another corner of sandwich on Peter's tray and let him get it first. He stuffed it into his mouth as if he was starving.

"See," said Ruth, rather smugly, "only you mustn't let him think you want him to eat it." She ate two more pieces herself before she let Peter grab another. "He watches you just like Josh does," she remarked, giving him a bit of cheese. "Good old Peter," she added, producing another when it was gone, "Have a bit more. Food tastes better when you have to fight for it!" and she ate a few of his crisps to prove her point.

"Try him with a whole sandwich."

Ruth gave him half, and he ate it in two starving bites

while she took a pretend swig out of his mug and passed it to Martin who obligingly took one too.

"Brilliant," said Martin, as Peter nearly suffocated himself draining it dry before they could get any more. Mrs Collingwood came home to the astonishing sight of a clean kitchen and her younger son clutching the last sandwich tight in both hands and glaring at Ruth as he consumed it.

"Darling, you're a hero, heroine, I should say!" she exclaimed. "Are you exhausted? Fancy you knowing how to feed him! And he's so clean," she added kissing Peter's bald head, "compared to usually I mean! You should see the sight he is when my poor Martin feeds him!"

"She did," said Martin, "we cleared it up."

"So useful," continued Mrs Collingwood, unstrapping Peter and turning him loose on the kitchen floor, where he grovelled round looking for crumbs, "if we could ask you again sometime. Martin hates it, poor pet, no stamina! What do you think? Say, a pound a tea, food thrown in, so to speak?"

Ruth stared at her, speechless. She had never imagined it would be so easy. Out of the corner of her eye she saw Martin watching her hopefully.

"Well, think it over," said Mrs Collingwood. "Could you stick it? It would only be now and then, say once or twice a week. Martin would be here, moral support, if nothing else! Do say yes!"

"Oh yes!" said Ruth.

"I'll have a talk with your mother; she won't mind, though. Right then, my Peter, bath time! Would you like to help, Ruth? Do you like babies?"

"No!" said Ruth hastily, "I mean yes, but it'll be teatime at home, I'd better go. Oh no," she added, seeing Mrs Collingwood reach for her purse, "today can be a free sample!"

"Rubbish," said Mrs Collingwood, gathering up Peter,

"I have to pay you, you might never come back otherwise!"

"I've got a job," announced Ruth happily at tea-time, "feeding Peter, a pound a meal!"

"Did you ask?" asked Mrs Conroy sternly, "or did they offer?"

"They offered," replied Ruth proudly, "they begged!"

"Ask if you have to wear your own clothes," said Mr Conroy solemnly, "I've seen that young man with an ice cream. Shocking!"

Naomi waited until she and Ruth were alone together before she said, "Do you realize that you will have to feed Peter more than a hundred times to get ten pounds a month for a year? That's once every three days! They'll never want you so often."

"There's pocket money too."

"There's all the birthdays this month."

"Home-made for Rachel and Phoebe," said Ruth firmly, "and flowers and we'll make a birthday cake for Mum to surprise her. She'll like that."

Mrs Conroy did like it, but when it came to Rachel's birthday, Rachel demanded explanations.

"What is it?"

"It's a sledge case!"

"I've never seen one before. There's no such thing!"

It looked like a huge cotton bag with straps. So that there should be no doubt as to its use, Ruth and Naomi had embroidered 'Sledge Case' on it in loopy chain stitch.

"I s'pose it's all right if it fits," said Rachel gracelessly.

"Of course it fits!" replied Ruth crossly. "D'you think we didn't measure? You might be more grateful; we sewed until our fingers bled, making it!"

"I don't want it if it's bled on," said Rachel.

"What are you going to get me?" asked Phoebe. "I don't want a sledge case!"

53

"Nothing if you're going to be as nasty as Rachel," said Naomi.

"I'm not being nasty," argued Rachel, "I'm being honest!"

Phoebe's turn to ask, "What is it?" came a few days later.

"It's a zoo keeper's hat!"

"What's the toothbrush for?"

"Cleaning out the cages."

"What's the cardboard animals for?"

"Putting in the zoo instead of us."

Phoebe let the cardboard animals loose in the garden and kept her relations in the cages.

"The Bigs have a secret," said Rachel, "a money secret!"

Phoebe was not interested. She was engrossed in writing a letter to Big Grandma.

> *Dear Big Grandma,* it said,
> *the 10 pond you give me is stuck in trane. By the slit it cannot breke it cost to much my trane.*
> *love Phoebe.*

"What does it mean?" asked Rachel, reading over her sister's shoulder.

"Can't you read?" asked Phoebe impatiently. "It says my ten pounds is stuck in the train and you can only get money in by the slit and it's no use saying I'll have to break the train because it's too valuable. So can she think of a way of getting it out."

"It doesn't say that at all," argued Rachel. "Anyway, listen to me. The Bigs have a secret. I think it's to do with money."

"They haven't got any money," pointed out Phoebe, "that's why they gave us such mingy birthday presents."

"What are you drawing?"

"My train."

"It can't be."

"It's a view through the slit, showing the money I can't reach."

"They're always upstairs counting money," continued Rachel, "and asking about my Christmas money. Good job they don't know where it is. I bet they'd steal it if they could."

"Where is it?" asked Phoebe. "Or have you lost it?"

"It's in a safe place," Rachel said. "I think," she added uncertainly, "I have to keep going to check."

Mrs Conroy had persuaded Rachel to deposit her money in a Post Office savings account. "A special children's one," Mrs Conroy had said. "They'll take care of it until you think of something special you really want."

"I really want another huge box of chocolates. Mine's gone already," Rachel had remarked incautiously, where upon Mrs Conroy had hurried her off to the Post Office round the corner, without further delay. The disadvantage of the system was that Rachel did not trust the Post Office staff.

"They've only given me this book," she said, scrutinizing her account. "They write in it themselves. They could write anything. How do I know they haven't spent it?"

Already Rachel's account book was filling up with a list of deposits and withdrawals, all for the same amount, as Rachel checked up on her money.

"She only wants to look at it," Mrs Conroy explained the first time Rachel dragged her back. Nevertheless, only four days after having deposited her money, before Rachel could hold it again in her hands, a form signed by Mrs Conroy and Rachel had needed to be filled in. Even then, Rachel, receiving her ten pound note, had taken one look and exclaimed,

"That's not mine! Mine was a new one and had a bent corner!"

"So it was," agreed the cashier, who at that time thought Rachel quite sweet, and he had replaced it with a new, bent-cornered one. After having examined it carefully, Rachel and her mother filled in another form and handed it back. Since then they had filled in so many forms that a separate pile was kept for Rachel and recently she had taken to popping in alone on her way back from school, in order to see the cashier wave a ten pound note at her to prove that, in her brief absence, he had not spent it.

"Catch the public young," the manager told his staff, "and you've got them for life." Whether or not they wanted Rachel for life was a different matter.

"Aren't you interested then?" asked Rachel.

"Everyone has money secrets," replied Phoebe. "Ruth and Naomi, Mum and Dad, everyone. You do."

"How do you know?" Rachel, alarmed, clasped the flat place on her stomach where her account book was warmly stowed between T-shirt and skin.

"I do know."

"Do you have money secrets too?"

Phoebe finished off her letter with a lot of kisses and did not reply.

"I hate it," said Rachel passionately, "when people have secrets. It's not fair, it makes me ill. I'm sure it's worse for me than other people. People ought to be made to tell me things."

"I showed you my letter."

"It was boring," said Rachel ungratefully. "Ruth and Naomi are upstairs writing boring letters too. Secret, boring letters."

"How do you know?"

"They won't let me in."

Joseck's letter had arrived the previous morning.

"It's taken weeks," said Ruth. "I ought to write back straight away if it's been so long coming."

"Look," said Naomi, "it was my money you sent as well, both of us should write, and we should tell him there's two of us, not just you."

"I thought you didn't want to share."

"I do now," said Naomi. Quite suddenly, the letter from Africa had brought Joseck alive. A real person, playing football, reading books and wondering why anyone would bother to sponsor him.

"Look, he's drawn a picture," said Ruth.

Sure enough, at the bottom of the page, in faint pencil lines, a dog chased a squirrel across the paper.

"Perhaps he saw one when he was writing."

> *Dear Joseck,* they wrote,
>   *Thank you for your letter. There are two of us, not just one. Ruth and Naomi. We are sisters. We are both well and we hope you are too. It is cold and wet and dark in our country. What books do you read? What animals are there in your country? We have read about Africa in books and we would like to go there. But it would cost too much. We thought if we had a friend in Africa we could write to them and they would write back. We thought we could go to Africa by post. That is why we sponsor you. To be our friend in Africa.*
> *Love from Ruth and Naomi.*

The letter filled the three picture postcards that Ruth had bought.

"We're supposed to keep the letters short," she said, "because they're in a foreign language to him, like us getting letters in French."

There was a thumping on the stairs and the door opened.

"Mrs Collingwood says would you stop with Peter for half an hour while she collects Martin from football?"

"Fifty pence," said Naomi.

"No, she always gives me a pound, even if it's only for half an hour. You go and post the letter."

"What letter?" asked Rachel, who had delivered Mrs Collingwood's message and lingered in the hope of discovering secrets. "What do you spend the money on?"

"Private."

"I've got a secret," said Rachel, "a money secret. Don't you want to know what it is?" and she was very pleased when Ruth and Naomi turned back eagerly to look at her.

"I knew you would," she remarked smugly, and disappeared down into the kitchen, where Mrs Conroy was making cakes for Sunday tea. A baking tray full of small chocolate buns stood on the kitchen table, waiting to go into the oven.

"I'd rather have one raw," said Rachel, looking at them, "than anything in the world. Than a hundred cooked ones! When will you have time to go to the Post Office with me?"

"Would you rather have one raw than go to the Post Office?" asked her mother. "Say, for a whole month?"

"For a week anyway."

"A month."

"Two weeks," said Rachel, edging towards the table.

"Three weeks."

"Three weeks then," agreed Rachel. "Do you think it will be safe that long?"

"Didn't you read that little book the man at the Post Office gave you? All about how they look after your money?"

"I read it in the bath."

"Yes?"

"But I dropped it in before I could believe it. That's why I have to keep checking."

"Well, you'll have to wait three weeks, now you've eaten that cake."

"Six weeks if you give me another," offered Rachel, and was ordered out of the kitchen.

Chapter Four

In the Post Office window there was a notice board, full of postcards. They advertised for sale such items as prams (as new), vacuum cleaners, and three-piece suites (buyer collects). There were also jobs.

'Experienced Nanny, also willing to cook and exercise dogs. Own car essential. Weekends and evenings as necessary. Typist preferred. References required.' That card had been there so long that it was brown at the edges, and so had the one that read, 'Cheerful young man to service, maintain and repair pensioner's car in return for occasional use.' Mr Conroy always said that it should not be called 'Situations Vacant' but 'Slave Labour'.

Naomi, pausing at the window after posting Joseck's letter, noticed a new card in the Slave Labour list:

'Reliable gardener required
2–3 hours per week
Tools provided
Previous applicant need not reapply.'

Naomi, wondering what the previous applicant had done to receive such a public rebuke, took down the address.

"How much d'you think gardeners get paid?" she asked Martin the next morning.

"Depends on their qualifications, I should think."

"If they haven't got any qualifications?"

"Well, depends on their experience then, I suppose."

"If they haven't any of that either?"

"Who'd employ them, then?" asked Martin practically.

"Somebody might," Naomi thought hopefully, and

that evening after school she cycled away to inspect the address. Nothing could have been more disheartening. A shabby red brick bungalow, surrounded by concrete paths and empty flower-beds. As Naomi looked, a curtain moved and a face appeared at the window.

"Looking for someone?" asked a voice behind her, and Naomi turned to see Mrs Reed, her old primary school headmistress.

"Naomi, isn't it?" she enquired. "Phoebe and Rachel's sister. I never forget a face! What are you doing here?"

"Just looking at the garden. It needs gardening."

"It certainly does," agreed Mrs Reed. "Nothing to redeem it, except that old apple tree."

For the first time, Naomi noticed a huge old apple tree that stooped across one corner of the garden. Beneath it was a garden shed, so old that the wood had weathered to a silver greyness.

"And the shed."

"Yes," agreed Mrs Reed, slightly surprised. "Anyway, I'm afraid it's all beyond the old couple these days."

The front door of the bungalow had opened and an ancient man, swaying between two sticks, made his way along the garden path towards them. He did not, Naomi noticed with disappointment, look rich.

"I see you looking," he called from half-way up the path, "and I knowed what you come for."

"To see the garden," explained Naomi, shouting in case he was deaf. "I saw your card in the Post Office."

"Are you one of Linda's?" he asked, looking across at Mrs Reed.

"One of mine grown up a bit," agreed Mrs Reed. "I didn't realize you were thinking of tackling the garden yourself, Naomi? Have you met Toby and Emma?"

"She've just met Toby," said Toby, smiling a toothless smile at Naomi, "and Emma's on her way. Emma's slowed down a bit these days," he continued, "she can't get about like she did. She'm dead set on having the garden planted up, though. Here she comes for a look."

Glancing behind him, Naomi saw an old lady progressing along the path with such small footsteps that she seemed to drift. The March breeze that chased last year's dead leaves in circles through the garden seemed more than likely to sweep her away with them. With a voice like paper in the wind she remarked,

"I was one of the first Girl Guides!"

"Oh," said Naomi, and then, rather stupidly, "why did you leave?"

Emma did not seem to find it a stupid question. "I wonder now," she admitted, "perhaps I shouldn't have rushed off."

"This young lady," announced Toby, "is our new gardener! And a cut above the last, if you ask me!"

"Cheeky young devil, him," remarked Emma.

"Well, it looks like you've got the job," said Mrs Reed to Naomi. "Do you want me to have a word with your mother? I've asked her to pop in for a chat sometime after school this week."

Naomi was staring in astonishment at the empty, dusky garden, the goblin figures of the old people, and Mrs Reed, who seemed to think there was nothing unusual in the situation.

"Pound an hour," said Toby, suddenly business-like, "no radios, no drinking, no smoking in the shed, no acting unreasonable, and no digging up of Roger!"

"Who's Roger?" asked Naomi, completely bemused.

"Him that come before," Emma told her, "dug him up!"

"Upset them terribly," said Mrs Reed. "Roger was their parrot!"

Suddenly Naomi realized that the garden had a third feature. Apple tree, silver shed, grave marked with a wooden cross.

"We could grow flowers on him," she suggested "parrot-coloured! Red and yellow and bright green and blue."

"Shallow-rooted," breathed Emma.

"One of Linda's," said Toby, who seemed to think a great deal of Mrs Reed. "One of Linda's got the job. Come back Saturday, any time Saturday."

"I'll speak to your mother," said Mrs Reed.

"Shallow-rooted," repeated Emma, wandering back to the house. "I was one of the first Girl Guides! Shallow-rooted, but nice and bright!"

Toby's hands were shaking on his sticks.

"Get into the warm," Mrs Reed ordered, as if he was six again. "You too, Naomi! I hope that bike has proper lights!"

Naomi nodded but did not move, waiting to see her employers safely indoors. Mrs Reed gave her arm a friendly pat.

"We'll all be old one day," she told her. "Well into their nineties, those two are. We'll be lucky if we're as bright as they are when it comes to our turn!"

Naomi, cycling home, thought about that.

"One day you'll be old," she told Phoebe when she got in.

"I shan't!"

"Ninety!"

"I won't!"

"Older than Big Grandma!"

Phoebe said nothing, but continued to scrub down Mrs Collingwood with her birthday toothbrush. Mrs Collingwood was the latest inmate of the zoo. She was having to share a cage with Rachel until Phoebe could find another box. "I told her I was a vegetarian and she called me a sausage!" Phoebe explained to Naomi.

"Where did you get the photograph?"

"I won't be old," said Phoebe. "Plasticine sausages for her tea. Serve her right!"

Rachel came wandering into the dining room and paused to inspect the zoo. "Mrs Collingwood in with me?" she asked, looking pleased and surprised and shy and excited all at the same time. "Brilliant! I hated being on my own!"

Naomi spent the evening reading gardening catalogues and making a list of all the red, yellow and blue plants that might be suitable for a parrot's grave.

"How deep is he buried?" asked Ruth, when the situation had been explained to her.

"Not very, I shouldn't think, if they had to dig the hole themselves."

"Wonder how long he's been dead," mused Ruth. "Pity to waste him, really!"

"If I dig up Roger for you," said Naomi sternly, "I'll get the sack!"

"Yes, all right," said Ruth hastily. "Probably too late anyway! Fancy you being a reliable gardener! You've only ever grown those radishes at Big Grandma's!"

"Well, she said they turned out very nicely," said Naomi. "Anyway, anyone can garden, thousands of books tell you how. It's not as bad as being a baby-sitter who's only practised on Phoebe! You can't look up babies in books!"

"You can," replied Ruth serenely, "I did in the library. There's all sorts of ways of bringing them up, timetables and discipline or give 'em what they like, all sorts of ways, depends what you want them to grow up like!"

"What do you do with Peter, then?"

"Whatever stops him screaming quickest," said Ruth.

Mrs Conroy met Mrs Reed as arranged and said very little when Mrs Reed brought up the subject of Toby and Emma. Starting back at the hospital had taken more of her time and energy than she ever thought it would. Her work was mostly in the evenings, and in between her leaving and Mr Conroy coming home was a worrying gap, filled by Naomi and Ruth getting tea. Lately Mrs Conroy's chief preoccupation seemed to be the cleanliness of Rachel and Phoebe. "Did Rachel and Phoebe come home from school clean? Sit down to tea clean? Go round to the Collingwoods clean?" And on the occasions when Ruth and Naomi saw their little sisters to bed, their mother would rush home and demand, "Did Rachel and Phoebe go to bed clean?"

(Naomi and Ruth had noticed that if they said 'Yes' she would hurry upstairs in disbelief to inspect them, but if they said 'No' she would sit peacefully down and remark that they could always be scrubbed in the morning.)

When Mrs Reed told her that Naomi had promised to do some gardening for a nice old couple she knew very well, Mrs Conroy had answered that she hoped Naomi would not get too dirty.

"Perhaps you'd like to go and see them," Mrs Reed had suggested, and Mrs Conroy replied that she would love to when she had time and added that she hoped Naomi wouldn't go making a nuisance of herself.

By Friday evening Naomi's plans were complete, and if all went as planned, Toby and Emma's red brick bungalow was well on the way to being transformed. Ruth, nobly sacrificing several nights' homework to a good cause, had painted pictures illustrating the blossomy paradise her sister intended creating. During spring and summer it could be seen that the bungalow would be entirely obscured, a mere form beneath the garlands of honeysuckle, roses and clematis. (Ruth had been very pleased when she discovered clematis; "Clematis Montana will even cover the roof!" she announced triumphantly.)

The autumn scene showed an odd brick or two peering coyly from between the late roses and Russian vine, but winter restored the old outlines completely, softened only by deep snow, ivy and glowing windows.

"There!" said Ruth, sucking her paint brush clean for the last time.

"There!" said Naomi on Saturday afternoon, plonking down Ruth's pictures on Toby's knee.

"We must be quiet!" whispered Toby, nodding across to the armchair where Emma lay sleeping, almost obscured by cushions and rugs. Creakingly, Toby rose and shuffled across the room to blot out Emma altogether with another piece of blanket.

"Bring them pictures," he told Naomi, and led her to the ice-cold kitchen. Naomi followed, after tiptoeing across the room to see that Emma had not been extinguished completely by her coverings. Toby sat at the kitchen table and carefully spread out the pictures before him.

"Well? What do you think?" asked Naomi.

"Very bright and pretty," said Toby eventually, "but to be honest my dear . . ." he glanced up and saw Naomi's face.

"If you'd ha' brought me these," he continued, "say, twenty, twenty-five years ago . . . (not that we lived here then) . . ."

"Where did you live?"

"Right out along the sea wall. I tell you, my dear, I tell you Ruth . . ."

"My name's Naomi," said Naomi crossly, "Ruth's my sister. She painted the pictures."

"She made a good job of them," agreed Toby, studying Ruth's signature. "Well, I tell you Naomi, twenty, twenty-five years ago I'd have snapped these pictures up and should we have lived here, and should Emma have wanted a garden so bad like she suddenly do now, I'd have planted the lot!"

"Good," said Naomi, "but what about now?"

"Twenty-five years ago," said Toby firmly.

"I wasn't here twenty-five years ago," said Naomi impatiently, "I was minus thirteen!"

"Emma and me was seventy each," Toby told her mildly. "I tell you frankly, my dear, these roses and trees take such a time to grow, you wouldn't believe."

There was a silence.

"Time you wouldn't believe," he repeated, as Naomi bundled the pictures together and marched towards the door.

"Well, why'd you want a gardener, then?" she demanded.

"What we need is fast flowers," continued Toby, producing a pencil and a bit of paper from the kitchen drawer. "Fast flowers! Straight from the packet and up in weeks! Annuals, you can scatter them anywhere and they flower all summer. What about that?"

"S'pose it's your garden," said Naomi ungraciously, "but I'd grow roses and honeysuckle and stuff."

"So would I," agreed Toby, "so would I. But you write these things down for me now. Six-week stocks and them nasturtiums that crawl everywhere and poppies aren't fussy, and them great big blue things that grow up quick and bright, you make a list and nip into town for the seeds and bang 'em in and there we are."

"What about Ruth's pictures?" asked Naomi, at the end of an afternoon spent choosing the fastest, brightest, toughest seeds in the seed catalogue.

"Emma would love a look at them," said Toby.

"Even though it won't look like that?"

"It will still look grand, just grand another way."

"All right," said Naomi.

"How did you get on?" Ruth, who had waited patiently for nearly an hour at the garden gate, pounced on her sister as she came out of the bungalow.

"He wants the garden packed full of flowers as soon as he can, any old flowers, so long as they're there. He liked your pictures but he said they would take too long."

"What's he done with them, then?"

"Stuck them up on the kitchen wall."

"Oh," said Ruth, as disappointed as Naomi had been, and she did not say anything else as they cycled home together.

"S'pose it's his garden," she admitted grudgingly, as they wedged their bikes into the garden shed. "Did you get paid?"

Naomi pulled a ten pound note from her pocket. "Three for me and the rest for seeds to get us started. I've got a list. I said I'd get them after school."

"Without charging him?" asked Ruth. "Why, what's the matter?"

Naomi, looking very worried, had hunched herself down on to the lawn-mower.

"Their bungalow," she explained, "freezing cold in the kitchen and dismal in the living room and everything old and bare, clean, but bare, nothing cheerful except your pictures, and Toby and Emma are old too, Emma looks nearly dead, I thought she was once, and he can't bend down and they walk so slowly . . ." she stopped speaking and stared at the ten pound note. "I don't think they can afford me. I don't like taking it."

Ruth lowered herself into a spidery corner, full of trowels and cobwebs and gnawed her knees in thought.

"It's all right for you. The Collingwoods are rich!" said Naomi.

"Too rich," said Ruth gloomily. "They're going away for Easter. Italy! Before it gets too crowded! No money for three weeks! And fancy taking Peter to Italy! What a waste! It's not fair."

"I wouldn't be seen dead with Peter in Italy," said Naomi.

68

"Neither would I," agreed Ruth, cheering up. "And you know if Toby and Emma want a garden, they have to pay someone. Might as well be you. Anyway, a pound an hour is very cheap, I bet. You cost less than the seeds!"

"S'pose I do."

"When I can, I'll come and help you and we'll still only be a pound an hour and they'll get even more money's-worth!"

Ruth scrambled to her feet and pulled Naomi out of the lawn-mower box. They trudged indoors, shedding cobwebs and grass cuttings all over the kitchen.

"Where have you been, to get like that?" asked Mrs Conroy.

"Sitting in the shed."

"Sitting in the shed!" repeated Mrs Conroy, "and Rachel has just come home covered in dog hairs and says she's been sitting in Josh's basket . . ."

"Only for a minute," interrupted Rachel.

"It only *took* a minute! Upstairs all of you and take the clothes brush! Where's Phoebe disappeared to?"

"Here," said Phoebe from beneath the kitchen table, where she had been studying Big Grandma's reply to her letter.

> *Dear Phoebe,* wrote Big Grandma,
>
> *Your train is worth more than ten pounds so if you break it you will be the loser. Therefore, until you have exhausted all possibilities do not break the train. At the moment the train and your money are both safe. I explained your difficulty to Graham and he suggested that you fish down the slit with very sticky chewing gum. He said Good Luck! Let us know how you get on!*
> *Love from Grandma (Big)*

Big Grandma's letter was as plain as Phoebe's had been obscure, and Graham had very kindly drawn a picture to illustrate how to fish with chewing gum. As a result, an afternoon's fishing had left Phoebe dreadfully entangled, and with no money at all to show for it. Mrs Conroy, regarding her hands and arms with disgust, ordered her upstairs with the rest of her daughters.

"Naomi, turn the taps on for her and make sure she doesn't touch *anything*!" she called after them, "and make her wash in cold water, hot just makes it worse! I told you to take no notice of that letter, Phoebe! Your grandmother is ridiculous at times!"

Rachel, waiting her turn while Ruth brushed Naomi, saw something fall from Naomi's pocket and pounced, but too late.

"Where did you get it?" she asked, as Naomi stuffed the ten pound note back into her jeans. An awful suspicion seized her and hastily she clasped her front and was reassured to find her Post Office book still there. Over the weeks it had softened and moulded so comfortably to the shape of Rachel's stomach that she could no longer feel it.

"Is it out of Phoebe's train?"

"WHAT!" exclaimed Phoebe, shooting, bright red and dripping, out of the bathroom.

"Of course it isn't," said Naomi, allowing Phoebe to examine the note, "look, yours was folded into squares; this one's just a bit screwed up. Anyway, how would I have got it out?"

"I don't know," admitted Phoebe, suddenly gloomy. "Chewing gum doesn't work." She unscrewed Big Grandma's letter and read it again.

"How will I know when all possibilities have been exhausted?"

"'Course you will know," said Rachel, surprised to find herself for once the cleverest, "your train will be all smashed to pieces!"

★　　★　　★

Toby was rather astonished the next Saturday to see that his gardening staff had suddenly doubled in size.

"Ruth's just come to read," Naomi explained, unloading a heap of library books from her bike basket. "We went to the library and got all these gardening books, so I'm going to garden and she's going to read the instructions."

"You're a bright lass to think of that," Toby told her approvingly. "There's the key to the shed, where you'll find the tools. I must go and get Emma started."

"Started?"

"Wrapped up, like, to come out and see you. She've been looking at those pictures you made all week."

He disappeared indoors, leaving Ruth and Naomi to explore the shed, select a spade and bucket, and begin the task of giving Toby his money's-worth.

"Preparation of the ground," read Ruth, sitting on the upturned bucket. "The ground should be made ready during the winter months . . ."

"Too late," said Naomi, "skip that bit."

"Liming and fertilizing . . ."

"We haven't got any, so you'll have to skip that too."

"Preliminary digging . . ."

"We haven't got time."

Ruth turned the pages until she came to 'Laying out a seed-bed, nursery beds and Accelerated seedling production'.

"I'm not bothering with all that," said Naomi, busily pulling weeds from around Roger's grave, "whatever it is, anyway. Find where you put the seeds in."

"It's three chapters," said Ruth, finding it and settling comfortably on her bucket to read. "It begins, 'One of the advantages of outdoor seed-beds is that they can be prepared and sown by semi-skilled staff . . .'"

"What a cheek," exclaimed Naomi, "Semi-skilled! Skip that bit!"

" 'The land must be free from weeds, especially the perennial kinds, such as nettles . . .' "

"I'm freeing it," said Naomi, sitting down hard, as a dandelion unplugged rather quickly. "Go on a bit!"

" 'If drainage is not good . . .' "

"Skip that, we couldn't do anything about it anyway."

" 'Autumn sowing', might as well skip that. What a useless book; I've skipped nearly all of it! You bash out the lumps while I pull the weeds up, that'll be twice as quick!"

By the time Toby and Emma appeared, they had finished one border and were ripping open packets of cornflowers and poppies and scattering the seeds.

"Save the marigolds for Roger," Naomi reminded Ruth, "and I bought some runner beans out of my own money, to climb up the wall behind him."

Emma, sitting on the chair Toby had brought out for her, nodded approvingly. "Nice and bright," she said, "but shallow-rooted! I don't forget!"

"No," said Naomi, extremely surprised.

"I was one of the first Girl Guides, you know," Emma continued, "I should never have left! You were right!"

"I was one of the last," said Ruth cheerfully.

"One of the last?"

"Well, I got thrown out!"

This remark startled Emma so much that she looked several years younger.

"Got thrown out?" she repeated.

"For bandaging," Ruth told her. "We had to do bandaging and I bandaged someone's legs together and bandaged them to the table . . ."

"Shut up!" whispered Naomi.

"Well, it was only Egg Yolk Wendy," said Ruth unrepentently, "and when I'd bandaged her to the table she went on and on so much I bandaged her mouth shut . . ."

Naomi glanced up from her weeding to see how Emma

was taking these remarks and then bent down again, reassured. Emma, sighing and bowing on the kitchen chair, appeared to be laughing.

Two weeks later the garden was transformed, dug and weeded and planted with seeds. Already, with not a single leaf or seedling showing, it looked a very different place from the neglected patch that Naomi had first visited. Between pocket money and Peter and gardening, Joseck's money had been earned twice over.

"We ought to keep the spare money for next month," said Ruth.

"We needn't," said Naomi airily, "we can always earn more. The Collingwoods will be back in a couple of weeks and that garden will always need gardening."

It was too tempting; it was so long since they had had any money to spend. The shops were full of Easter eggs; in one you could wait while they iced a person's name on the egg of your choice. Egg Yolk Wendy off the school bus, clutching the unfortunate Gavin by the arm, was waiting in the queue.

"Gavin's getting my name put on an egg," she told them, smirking.

"Poor you," remarked Ruth "can't you stop him?"

"Not very kind of you, Gavin," added Naomi. "Good job nobody's seen you except us. We won't tell anyone."

"I suppose," said Ruth, "it's nothing actually to be ashamed of."

Wendy let go of Gavin's arm and looked at him uncertainly.

"Personally," said Naomi, "I'd rather wear a dog collar and be done with it!"

"Or a ball and chain," agreed Ruth, watching Gavin edge towards the door, "or mittens on a string through the arms of my coat."

Gavin, hovering on one leg in the doorway, watched his rescuers hopefully.

"We've come to get one done for our little sisters," explained Ruth. "Rachel's too old really, but she only sulks if she doesn't get the same as Phoebe."

"She's immature," said Naomi, but Wendy had suddenly disappeared.

Ruth moved to the front of the queue and said, "We want one egg with Mum and Dad on it please, and another with Rachel written on one half and Phoebe on the other."

"It'll look all wrong in the box."

"They won't care about the box," said Naomi cheerfully. "And one of those little pink rabbits with Gavin on please!"

"We don't normally ice rabbits," said the girl, "but I'll do it anyway for a favour! That poor lad! I was watching through the window. She counted his money and dragged him in!"

"I wonder," said Naomi as they walked home, "if they have Easter in Africa."

"Well, they have Christmas."

"They must have, then. Look! There's Gavin and Wendy! Give me that rabbit!"

Ruth handed it to her, and distracted Wendy by the simple remark, "Your hair's growing out at the roots," while Naomi planted the rabbit in Gavin's school bag, where it was discovered with rage and suspicion by Wendy the next morning.

"I bet they don't have chocolate Easter eggs though," continued Naomi as if no interruption had occurred. "I wonder if he's got our letter yet? I wish they didn't take so long to get there."

"Perhaps he's reading it now," said Ruth, guessing exactly right.

The letters had been handed round the class that morning and Joseck's face grew brighter and brighter as he read his.

"Now we have to write back," said Mari crossly. She had a letter too, full of questions about her home and school and family. This was unfortunate, because Mari was famous in the school for never answering questions if she could possibly avoid doing so.

"I have two people now," said Joseck, "and they want me to be their friend in Africa."

"You can't," said Mari.

"I can."

"You should write 'I cannot be your friend in Africa. It is too far away'," Mari told him sternly. "I'm not writing anything to my lady. I'm drawing a picture."

"You did that before."

"Yes, and she says she liked it and stuck it on her wall."

"She doesn't need another, then."

"She must have more than one wall."

Joseck shrugged his shoulders to signify that it was no use arguing with Mari.

He wrote,

> *Dear Ruth and Naomi,*
>
> *I am your friend in Africa.*
>
> *I am very glad. The animals we have are twelve goats my father has and there are some cattle. In the hills are deer and small cats and plenty of animals. The books I read are all the books the school has. Here it is also cold at night. We have the fire and my father sometimes tell us stories. What are you doing in your country? Here we have already harvested beans. The boys in my class play football and Mari comes to play too. She is too small and we say no but she comes still.*
>
> *I am very happy to receive your letter.*
>
> *Your friend in Africa,*
>
> *Joseck.*

Helped tremendously by the teacher, Mari had written,
> *Thank you for the letter.*

Underneath she had drawn a picture of a frowning man with eyes like stones.

"That is not very nice," said the teacher.

"It is you," said Mari, very cheerful because the letter writing was nearly over.

"Your lady will think it is you," said Joseck, so Mari's letter said,
> *Thank you for the letter. This is not me.*

Chapter Five

Rachel and Phoebe woke up at five o'clock on Easter Sunday morning and discovered, to their huge delight, that the Easter bunny had rashly left his presents on the end of their beds.

"Which will never happen again," announced Mrs Conroy later that disastrous day.

"*We* were all right," pointed out Rachel.

Between five o'clock and half-past six that morning, Rachel and Phoebe consumed three large chocolate eggs, one packet of marzipan ducks, one packet of peppermint cream rabbits, three bananas stolen from the kitchen for no good reason that Rachel could give, two hard-boiled eggs, painted pink with their names on, and two cooking apples, raw, because they were thirsty. Strengthened by their efforts, and finding there was nothing left to eat, they got up and went to see how Ruth and Naomi were getting on.

Naomi was lying very curled up on the edge of her bed, clutching the pillow with one hand and looking strangely pale.

"Happy Easter!" said Rachel, bouncing on to her feet, "thanks for your Easter egg, we ate half each. Here's yours from me, home-made at school," and she pulled an oily parcel from her pyjama jacket pocket. "We could do six little ones or one big one so I did you one big one! And Phoebe made one for Ruth."

"Where is Ruth?" demanded Phoebe. "She didn't find her Easter egg. I hid it for a surprise up Old Teddy's jumper and it's still there!"

"She must have slept with it all night," remarked Rachel. "Is it squashed?"

"Just a bit melted!"

Naomi had unwrapped her parcel and was gazing at a large grey fondant egg, splashed all over with paintbox-red dots.

"We painted them last night," said Rachel complacently, "Ruth's got yellow stripes. Why haven't you eaten anything yet?"

"Stop talking about food," said Naomi, "Were you, Ruth?" she continued as Ruth pushed the door open and collapsed on to her bed.

"Was she what?" asked Rachel.

"Sick."

"No," said Ruth.

"We've eaten all our Easter stuff," Rachel said, "we had a feast, we didn't mean to, but then it didn't seem worth stopping so we ate the hard-boiled eggs and ducks and rabbits from Big Grandma to finish off!"

Ruth pulled her pillow over her head.

"And bananas," said Phoebe, cheerfully pulling it off again. "Look under Old Teddy's jumper, Ruth. I've put a surprise!"

"Something in this room smells disgusting," said Ruth, not listening. "Really sweet and disgusting, I've been smelling it all night." She paused and watched in horror as Naomi, bracing herself, took a bite of her fondant egg.

Phoebe lost patience and banged Old Teddy down on Ruth's stomach so hard that he laid an egg, yellow and damp and rather hairy. It was suddenly too much for Ruth.

"Where are they?" asked Mrs Conroy, coming in a few moments later to see what all the noise was about.

"Both in the bathroom," Rachel told her.

"What have they been eating?"

"Nothing, well, Naomi ate a bit of the Easter egg we made her. Ruth wouldn't even look at hers, she shouted,

78

'Get it out of my bed! Get it out of my bed!' and ran to the bathroom, and so did Naomi!"

"I'll eat it," offered Rachel as Phoebe stooped and retrieved Ruth's egg from where it had rolled, under the bookcase. "I've eaten Naomi's so it can't be the paint."

"What paint?"

"The paint I put the dots on with; I was checking whether it was poisonous but it can't be because I'm all right!"

Except for a temporary loss of appetite at breakfast time, Rachel and Phoebe continued to be all right. Ruth and Naomi spent the day in bed and Mr Conroy remarked that there was no justice in this world.

"Tummy upsets," said Mrs Conroy on Sunday evening. Rachel visited the invalids on Monday morning and returned looking very pleased with herself.

"I've taken their Easter eggs to look after," she told Phoebe.

"Do they know?" asked Phoebe.

"I didn't tell them because they hate talking about food so much."

The doctor came on Tuesday and said, "Gastric flu. Lucky the other two have escaped."

"Escaped what?" asked Rachel.

"Catching what your big sisters have gone down with."

"You can't catch paint, can you?" asked Rachel, who had witnessed Naomi's sufferings very guiltily for the last two days.

"Stick your tongue out," ordered the doctor, who was an old friend of Rachel's. "Give me your wrist, say 'Ah', jump up and down a bit, tell me the alphabet as fast as you can."

"Aybeecee dee ee efgee ach i jaykayellem en oh peekew are esstee you veedouble you ex why zed, am I all right?" demanded Rachel.

"Sound as a bell, but talking rubbish," said the doctor,

handing Mrs Conroy a sheaf of prescriptions. "And how's Phoebe, the wonder child? Still top of the class?"

"Yes," said Phoebe, not very modestly. "I'm learning handstands and chess now."

"Both together?"

Phoebe explained that she did the handstands in between moves while waiting for her opponents to make their minds up and added that she almost invariably won.

"Do you think I have gastric flu?" she asked.

"Not noticeably," said the doctor.

"How much longer do you think it's going to last?" asked Naomi wearily on Thursday. Her head was hot and thumping and her back was shaking cold and when she tried to write a note to Toby she found herself going dizzy.

> *Dear Toby and Emma,* she wrote,
>   *I am sorry we have not been but we have flu.*
> *Will come as soon as we can, love Naomi and Ruth*

It took her all afternoon, in bits and pieces, to write. Ruth, staggering out of bed to look for a stamp, suddenly slipped and bashed her head on the window-sill.

"Are you getting better?" asked Rachel, through a crack in the door.

"I don't think so," said Ruth. "Will you post a letter for us?"

"Has it got germs on?"

"Probably."

"Wait," commanded Rachel, and came back wearing her winter mittens as protection.

"The doctor said it wasn't the paint," she said, grabbing the letter and going back to speak through the crack in the door.

"No, I know."

"And Phoebe's egg up Old Teddy's jumper couldn't have made Ruth as sick as this."

"No."

"I'm sorry," said Rachel, "but we've sort of eaten your Easter eggs."

"All of them?"

"Not the wrappers."

"Oh well," said Ruth, "we knew you probably would. Go and borrow Josh, so Martin doesn't forget he said we could share him, and post this letter for us."

"Poor Josh is in kennels."

"Oh yes, I forgot."

Rachel wandered off to the letter-box feeling lonely. Even more than she missed Ruth and Naomi, she missed Josh. He had been incarcerated in kennels while the Collingwoods went to Italy, and as a result Phoebe had confined the entire family in as terrible conditions as she could devise, in an outdoor extension of the zoo.

"Zoos don't have dungeons," Rachel had objected, when Phoebe had invented it.

"Mine does," replied Phoebe, who got a great deal of pleasure out of digging up their cage and seeing how soggy they were getting.

By the weekend Ruth and Naomi had progressed to dry toast and orange juice and could sit up and read without feeling that their heads might explode at any minute. Ruth had lost eight pounds and Naomi six, and it was another week before they could stagger downstairs and manage scrambled eggs for tea.

"You look a pair of little ghosts," remarked Mr Conroy.

"Do you mind about us eating your Easter eggs yet?" asked Rachel, but they were still far from well enough to regret the loss of anything sweet.

"You've wasted all the holidays," remarked Phoebe, "school again on Monday."

"Not for these two," said their mother. "They're going

up to Grandma's for a few days of fresh air! I must get back to work and they're still far from fit for school; they'd pick up the first thing that was going around."

"It's not fair," said Rachel bitterly that afternoon in the garden. "You Big Ones always leave me and Phoebe out of everything!"

"We don't!"

"You do. You're getting all stuck-up and bossy. Aren't they, Phoebe?"

Phoebe looked up from her re-interring of the Collingwoods. "Like Egg Yolk Wendy," she agreed dispassionately.

"WE'RE NOT!"

"You didn't care that we ate your Easter eggs! You had gastric flu without us and now you're going to sneak off to Big Grandma's and we'll be left behind! You even write letters to people we don't know, and," concluded Rachel, gratified to find that real tears of frustration were rolling down her cheeks, "you've had a huge, great big money secret without us for ages now! It's not fair!"

Naomi stared at Rachel in amazement and remarked briefly that she was cracked.

"Yes, you are," agreed Ruth. "We're only going to Big Grandma's because we had gastric flu. You could have come and caught it if you'd wanted to! You never came near us, except to pinch our Easter eggs! You would only speak to us through the crack in the door!"

"I didn't know about missing school and going to Big Grandma's then," said Rachel, sniffing.

"And how do you know we've got money secrets? And if we had, why should we tell you? You'd tell everyone and you wouldn't help!"

"I would!" Another tear trickled down Rachel's face and she wiped her nose on her knees and tried to look pathetic.

"You would what?" asked Naomi suddenly. "Help? Or tell everyone?" Once again she and Ruth were worrying about Joseck's money. It was obvious that very little, if any, could be earned that month. Two weeks had gone already and all their savings had been spent.

"I wouldn't tell anyone," said Rachel hopefully, "I would help. Promise!"

"Promise for ever?"

"Promise for ever," agreed Rachel, her tears drying up like magic.

"What about you, Phoebe?"

"I'll promise not to tell anyone," agreed Phoebe, who never told anyone anything anyway, "but," she added cautiously, "I don't promise to help!"

"Typical," said Naomi. "Anyway, all it is, is me and Ruth have bought an illegal boy in Africa and we pay for him to go to school, you do it through an agency, ten pounds a month, and we write to him and he writes back to us. He's our friend, we've got his photograph and we could go and visit him, only we haven't any money."

"Why is he illegal?" interrupted Phoebe.

"Because you have to be over eighteen and Ruth wrote a thirteen that looked like an eighteen but no one will ever find out if we keep sending the money. But we've run out of money. What did you do with your Christmas ten pounds, Rachel?"

"It's a secret," said Rachel, clutching her dilapidated front.

"You've spent it!"

"I haven't!"

"Good. Well, the boy's name is Joseck. He's very nice and very poor . . . "

"I am terribly poor," interrupted Rachel, "except for my ten pounds."

"Real truly poor, hardly any proper clothes and sometimes not enough to eat."

"No one could call our clothes proper," remarked Phoebe.

"Sometimes," said Rachel pathetically, "I think I have hardly enough to eat."

"What will happen if you don't send the money, then?" asked Phoebe. "I mean, except for Ruth getting arrested for saying she was eighteen?"

"Oh, thank you for caring," said Ruth.

"We don't know," Naomi said. "They might stop him going to school, we think, because of us not paying. Then he won't get his school dinner, and anyway he will feel awful. Disappointed. He thinks we're his friends."

"School dinners are horrible," said Rachel comfortingly, "so is school. He won't care."

"They're the best food Joseck gets, and he likes school, he's clever. I bet he'd be miserable."

"You have to send his money," said Phoebe firmly, "or else you will be mean pigs and I will bury you with the Collingwoods and put worms in your cage!"

"But we've run out of money. We spent it all on Easter eggs, and then we got ill so we couldn't earn any more and now we've got to go to Big Grandma's," Ruth said.

"Well, me and Rachel will help," said Phoebe grandly, but rather rashly. "Rachel's promised to, anyway," she added, ignoring Rachel's alarmed expression. "You should have asked us before!"

Two days later found Rachel staring at the envelope Ruth and Naomi had left and feeling completely unheroic.

"It's addressed and got a stamp on and everything," Ruth had said. "All you have to do is put a ten pound postal order inside, or a ten pound note if that's easier."

Nothing was easy about the task. If Phoebe had not interfered, if Joseck's school dinners had not been the best food he ever had, if Rachel's conscience had been untroubled by the thought of all the Easter eggs she had consumed, if all these things had not happened, Rachel would never have agreed to help. However, it was too late now; Ruth and Naomi were gone, Rachel had promised, and Phoebe's train had refused to yield its riches. 'I suppose,' thought Rachel, wriggling with horror at the thought, 'I shall have to rob the Post Office.' It was the only solution she could think of, and because the robbing of the Post Office seemed less appalling than the contemplation of the thought, she stowed Joseck's envelope in her usual hiding place and set off at a nervous trot to commit the crime.

There was a queue at the counter. One position was closed, and at the other, where Rachel's tame cashier was sitting, two old ladies waited to draw their pensions. The cashier recognized Rachel at once and cheerfully waved a ten pound note at her. Pretending not to notice, Rachel lined up behind the old ladies. It would have been comforting to be in disguise, but then the whole success of Rachel's plan depended on the fact that the cashier would know who she was. The first old lady moved away and Rachel's hands tightened on her quaking stomach.

'It isn't really crime,' she thought, feeling most unburglarish, "It's my money. It's not my fault they won't give it to me without a grown-up. They should have told me that, before I put it in. I never would have then, they're the burglars, not me. I'm only getting it back. It's my money!" She found herself standing at the counter and realized she had spoken aloud.

"Of course it is," agreed the cashier. "Did you think I'd spent it? There you are," and he slapped a ten pound note down on his side of the counter.

"That's not mine," said Rachel, determined to take only what was her own. "You know it isn't. Mine was much newer and had a bent corner."

"How could I have forgotten?" asked the cashier,

reaching down and producing a new, bent-cornered one. "There it is!"

Rachel's hand, damp and grubby and cold with fear but small enough to achieve her purpose, shot beneath the grille, grabbed the ten pound note, and the next moment she was running, running as fast as she could, down the street, round the corner towards her school, to the letter-box that stood by the school gates. Here she paused and looked back. She had expected to be pursued but no one had given chase. Hastily she retrieved the envelope from her front, stuffed the ten pound note inside and posted it.

'Now Joseck's safe!' she thought, and the feeling of relief and achievement was so great that she hugged herself with delight. A second later her happiness left her. If Joseck was safe it was equally certain that she, Rachel, certainly wasn't. Why hadn't the cashier run after her, she wondered? Or perhaps he had, but she had run too fast. Perhaps he had simply called the police and they were at her home, waiting for her, or tracking her footsteps with Alsation dogs on leads. Rachel looked down at her dusty trainers and wondered if she should take them off, to baffle the dogs. It seemed a sensible idea.

Cautiously, in her socks, she retraced her footsteps to the corner and looked round. There was the Post Office, she could see the red and yellow sign, but nobody was outside looking for her. Except for two small boys on bikes and a tortoiseshell cat, the street was empty.

"Trod in something?" asked one of the boys, eyeing her socks, as Rachel crept along the road.

No policemen waited for her outside the Post Office. Rachel, tiptoeing past the door, listened for the sound of voices, unaware that inside, the manager and the cashier were laughing and laughing. They had not called the police, or prepared an ambush or given chase because they had another plan. It was to have a word with Rachel's mother.

Weak with relief, Rachel reached her home and noticed with satisfaction that no police vans were parked outside. It looked unbelievably normal. Her mother was potting up seedlings in the shed.

"I've grown far too many," she remarked to Rachel, not seeming to notice that her daughter had turned into a criminal. "Perhaps Naomi will take a few to her old people when they get back."

It was as if the past hour had been a dream. Mr Conroy sat in his usual chair, reading gloomily through a pile of bills.

"Where's Phoebe?" asked Rachel.

"Upstairs, as far as I know."

Phoebe was sitting on her bunk, looking very guilty. As Rachel entered, she jumped and stuffed something under her pillow.

"I've robbed the Post Office," said Rachel.

"I've broken my train," said Phoebe.

There was a small silence while they glared at each other.

"You'll get in awful trouble," said Rachel, not without a certain amount of satisfaction.

"So will you."

Side by side they sat on Phoebe's bunk and contemplated the tattered remains of the Post Office book, and the shattered china of Phoebe's train.

"Just proves," remarked Rachel eventually, "how stupid it is to save money. I never will again. Look what happens!"

"Was it hard, robbing the Post Office?" enquired Phoebe presently.

"Terrible. Horriblest thing I've ever done."

Phoebe, remembering with awe all the horrible things Rachel had ever done, things which included setting fire to Big Grandma's house and being accidently sick into someone else's desk ("Well, at least it wasn't your own," Naomi had remarked at the time) shuddered in sympathy.

"You needn't have done it, now I've broken my train."

"You needn't have broken your train now I've robbed the Post Office."

"Listen!" said Phoebe.

Downstairs there was a sudden clamour of voices, Mrs Conroy's raised, exclaiming, and Mr Conroy's and at least one stranger's.

"Rachel!" shouted Mrs Conroy up the stairs. "I think you've got some explaining to do, young lady!"

"Come with me and stop me telling them," begged Rachel, "before they come up here and see your train."

"Just keep saying sorry," advised Phoebe, and "Sorry I robbed the Post Office!" said Rachel over and over again, to her dissatisfied parents and the Post Office manager who had arrived and related Rachel's crime, as soon as the Post Office had closed.

Nothing could persuade her to say any more, to explain why she had done it, or how she had disposed of the money. Backed staunchly by Phoebe, she repeated that she was sorry, she wished she hadn't, and she never would do it again.

"Try and cry a bit," suggested Phoebe, in a whisper that was unfortunately overheard. She was sent from the room, and Rachel, without her support, really did manage to burst into tears—loud, noisy roaring ones, drowning the sound of all further questions.

"What are you doing to her?" enquired Phoebe, returning to the room after concealing the remains of her train.

"Nobody is doing anything to her," said Mrs Conroy crossly, and eventually they gave up and sent her to bed, where she slept soundly and awoke to a day of bright sunshine and the cheerful thought that the worst was over.

"You're in disgrace," her father told her.

"I know," agreed Rachel, staring at her knees, but she did not feel disgraced. She felt noble.

'I am brave,' she thought, 'so are you,' she silently told her knees, 'you helped run away!'

"We've got a friend in Africa," Rachel told her knees. "One day we'll go there!"

Chapter Six

Two days after Ruth and Naomi arrived in Cumbria, a grubby envelope was delivered to them.

> *Dear R and N,* wrote Phoebe,
> > *We have don it now.*
> *Love Phoebe.*

Underneath this unreassuring remark Phoebe, using an enormous amount of black pencil and spit, had drawn a detailed and dramatic picture of recent events in Lincolnshire. Even by Phoebe's standards the illustration was complicated, and realizing this the artist had carefully added footnotes.

'Rachel' she had written on one side of the picture, and 'prizon' on the other. 'Do not xplane this to B G' she had added as an afterthought.

"She's put Rachel in her zoo," guessed Naomi.

"Rachel's in it already," Ruth pointed out, "and what about 'We have done it now'? She might mean anything!"

"Do not explain this to Big Grandma," repeated Naomi, "as if anyone could!"

There was a day of anxious waiting and then another letter arrived, this time from Rachel.

> *Dear Ruth and Naomi,*
> > *I hope you are having a nice time, I wish I was there too. Even for gastrick floo. Phoebe says she wrote and told you about me having to rob the post office but I*

never told anyone why but I said you mite have made me, that is all. It is alright now but Im not going in again to buy stamps so I know you shouldnt but they get there anyway.

    Love Rachel.

Ruth, who had been forced to part with nearly a whole week's pocket money to secure this masterpiece, groaned, and handed it to Naomi.

"Well, it's perfectly clear," said Naomi, "Rachel's robbed the Post Office so she doesn't want to go in and buy stamps, probably feels awkward, so she posted this without one and you had to pay eighty pence instead."

"I can understand that bit," answered Ruth. "What I can't understand is why Rachel robbed the Post Office and how it can be all right if she did and what Phoebe's picture meant and why she said we sort-of made her and who the prison was for."

"I don't feel safe these days," said Naomi. "I wish we hadn't told them and then had to come away."

"People who feel safe," remarked Big Grandma, appearing from nowhere, "are usually mistaken. Sorry to make you jump like that! You people are very tense this week, I've noticed!"

> *Dear Ruth and Naomi,* said a postcard from Mrs Conroy,
>   *I do hope you are feeling better now. We will be glad to have you back. Goodness knows what the Little Ones have been up to lately, I'm afraid Rachel has been very naughty but that is all over now. The inevitable has happened and Phoebe has broken her little train. Dad says see you on Sunday! Love from both of us,*
>   *Mum and Dad.*

"Poor old Phoebe!" said Ruth. "They must have used her train money for Joseck."

"Must have done," agreed Naomi, "I wonder what Rachel's been up to, and I'm worried about Toby and Emma. We'll have missed four Saturdays."

"Write to them," suggested Ruth.

> *Dear Toby and Emma,*
> *We are nearly better now so we will be coming back as soon as we can so do not get anyone else. I hope you are well. Love Naomi.*

> *Dear Girls,* came back a reply by return of post,
> *Don't you worry yourselves my dears your flowers are all through fighting fit.*
> *Toby.*

Lovely as springtime was in Cumbria, a feeling of urgency began to grow on Ruth and Naomi.

"We ought to get back," said Ruth. "A letter might arrive from Joseck. I never thought to tell those two to watch the post."

"They might be telling anyone anything, at least Rachel might."

"I've a feeling you'll be glad to go home," said Big Grandma surprisingly on their last day.

"Not glad," said Ruth, "but we've got things we ought to do."

"We love it here," said Naomi, "you know we do, but . . ."

"But . . ." said Big Grandma. "Quite. Your faces are very revealing! Perhaps you'll tell me about it one day!"

"About what?" asked Ruth, but Big Grandma merely grinned at her and remarked that she was not so green as she was cabbage-looking.

★　　★　　★

"I wonder," said Ruth on the train home, "what Big Grandma knows."

"About Joseck?" asked Naomi. "How can she know anything? The trouble with Big Grandma is that she doesn't forget things. She notices everything and it goes into her head and makes patterns. Or something. So the more she notices, the more she knows."

"Good job, then, that she lives so far away," said Ruth heartlessly.

"Yes, lucky Mum's not like her!"

"Or Dad."

"Phoebe's bad enough!"

"Phoebe!"

"Well, she thinks just like Big Grandma," Naomi pointed out, and Ruth was silent, appalled at the thought of two Big Grandmas, or even worse, two Phoebes in the same family.

Mr Conroy was waiting for them on the platform as they drew into the home station; he nodded and smiled as the train pulled in, but could not wave because his hands were full of Rachel and Phoebe. He held them by the scruffs of their necks to prevent them from hurling themselves under the train.

"Rachel's looking nearly ready to burst," commented Ruth.

Rachel was exploding with questions and secrets. Joseck and robbery conflicted with the excitement of Ruth and Naomi's return, and the desire to know what they had brought her, and how many people in Cumbria regretted her being left behind.

"Did anyone say they wished I was there?" she asked, peering hopefully into a carrier bag of spring cabbages from Big Grandma's garden. "Has anyone given you anything to give to me? Did you get my letter?"

Phoebe asked no questions, watching detached and

unruffled as Mr Conroy hugged the travellers and Rachel rifled through their luggage. However, as they left the platform, she remarked,

"Everything's all right in Africa."

"Is it?" asked Ruth, immensely relieved. "Everything all right?"

"Only in Africa," said Phoebe, not wishing to raise her sister's hopes too much. "I told Big Grandma to tell you, when she telephoned this morning, but she said you'd already gone."

"Gone where?"

"On to the train home, to here. She was ringing to say you caught it all right. I answered the phone. She said you were worried about something so I said to tell you everything was all right in Africa, but then she said you'd gone."

"What else did she say?"

"Nothing," said Phoebe, "only, 'Good old Phoebe'."

"We came home just in time!" A letter from Joseck arrived in the morning, the letter that he had written describing the goats and the deer and the small cats in the hills.

"What sort of cats?" wondered Rachel. "Lions? Lions are cats."

"They're not small, though," pointed out Ruth, but Rachel said perhaps Joseck was so used to living in Africa, and lions and being boiling hot all day, that lions seemed ordinary. "And small," she concluded. "I'll write and ask him. He's my friend too, now. It was my ten pounds."

"What about me?" asked Phoebe. "What about my train? I was going to send him my train money. I didn't know that Rachel had gone to rob the Post Office!"

"No one possibly could," said Naomi. "Only Rachel could think of anything so stupid. Or do something so stupid."

"It was very brave of me," said Rachel. "You and Ruth couldn't think of anything except being sick."

"There are books in the library on Africa," Ruth hastily changed the subject. "We could go after school and look up African animals. And he's all our friend now, so we'll all write back. He'll be glad to have four, I expect."

The library was well stocked with African books, and the girls had four tickets each, so they chose sixteen between them, which left a very large gap in the section.

"You'll know your way round by the time you get there," remarked the librarian, as he stamped the sixteenth.

"How did you know we were going?" asked Rachel.

"Just guessed."

"Pity we couldn't, really," said Ruth as they walked home, laden.

"Why couldn't we?"

"Costs too much."

"We could save up," said Phoebe.

That evening, in the gap when Mrs Conroy had gone to work and Mr Conroy had not yet come home, they composed a joint letter to Joseck.

"Let Naomi write it," suggested Ruth who was cooking tea for everyone. "She's the neatest."

> *Dear Joseck,* wrote Naomi,
>   *Now there are four of us. Me and Ruth and Rachel and Phoebe who are our sisters. They are seven and . . .*

"Nearly ten," said Rachel.

"Nine and two months isn't nearly ten," said Naomi, "I'll put nine."

"Ask who Mari is?" said Ruth.

> *Seven and nine,* wrote Naomi.
>   *Who is Mari? Ruth wants to know. She cannot write because she is cooking . . .*

"Beans on toast," said Rachel happily, "tell him that."

"He might not know what toast is; it doesn't sound very African."

She is cooking beans and bread. We have got sixteen books about Africa with pictures of deer and cats like you said. Rachel says do you ever see lions, she thinks Africa is full of lions. In our country it is spring, we have planted seeds and there are lambs where our Big Grandma lives. But no goats. Lambs are baby sheep.

"Tell him Ruth is burning the bread," suggested Phoebe, and Ruth dashed across the room and seized the blackened toast from under the grill.

Ruth is burning the bread, wrote Naomi obligingly, Rachel is scraping the black off. Phoebe is saving up to come and see you, she says. I wish we really could. It is strange to think this piece of paper is going all the way to Africa and you will read it.

"Why did you put that?" asked Rachel.

"Because it is strange," replied Naomi. "I can hardly believe it."

"If a piece of paper can go," said Phoebe, "I don't see why we can't."

Love from Ruth and Naomi and Rachel and Phoebe.

A little baked bean juice got on to the paper as they all signed their names.

"Fancy our baked bean juice going to Africa!" said Rachel.

"Now what?" asked Rachel, having watched (from a safe distance) the ceremonial posting of Joseck's letter.

"Now get thinking," said Naomi, "because we've got to get more money."

"There's still Phoebe's ten pounds."

"I'm saving that to go to Africa," Phoebe interrupted. "It's fair. I'm saving up for all of us to go, not just me."

"Where are you keeping it this time?"

"In Mrs Collingwood's cage," replied Phoebe, "because

she's the richest person I know. I thought she'd be the best at looking after it."

"Is it still buried in the garden?" asked Ruth, alarmed.

"I dug it up when they came back from Italy," explained Phoebe, "and I took out Mr Collingwood and Martin because they'd gone mouldy and I let Peter out because he's useful."

"Peter useful?"

"For making money out of," said Phoebe.

"Peter might not last much longer," said Ruth gloomily, remembering the scene she had witnessed only the day before. Mrs Collingwood had called her proudly into the kitchen as she returned after borrowing Josh.

"You'll appreciate this," Mrs Collingwood had said, and Ruth had watched in horror as Peter, perfectly clean and civilized, had rammed toast soldiers into a boiled egg, consumed them with only minimal damage to his attire and surroundings, and washed them down with gulps of milk.

"Fascinating, you've got to admit," said Mrs Collingwood. "Well worth going to Italy for. A kind waiter in the hotel trained him!" She disappeared to answer the phone, and Ruth, with great presence of mind, picked up the empty egg shell and showed Peter how to smash it flat on his tray.

"Good Peter!" she said, watching as with happy fists, he pounded it to fragments. She felt very guilty as Mrs Collingwood returned to the devastation, especially when Peter, beaming at his mother, announced that he was a Good Peter. She could see that nothing but the power of speech prevented Peter from explaining his new accomplishment. Still, she had Joseck in Africa to think of; Peter could not be allowed to grow up too quickly.

"What else could I do?" she asked her sisters. "Goodness knows what else that waiter taught him!"

"Peter likes smashing things up," said Naomi. "It's

kindness really, to show him how. He'll never have such good chances when he's grown up. When are you going back?"

"Thursday after school. Mrs Collingwood said could I amuse him for a couple of hours while she cooks, because they're having a dinner party."

"I wish we had our dinner at night," murmured Rachel dreamily, "you could eat as much as you liked and then not have to do anything but lie down flat."

"Perhaps," said Naomi, "it would be a good idea if every time you went, you taught him something really aggravating to do."

"No, I can't do that," said Ruth. "It really wouldn't be fair. Anyway, he's learning to talk more every day, he might tell. I'll just not teach him anything useful, especially not English. Lucky that waiter only spoke Italian to him, so that's all he's learned!"

"Italian!"

"Oh yes, he says 'hello' and 'goodbye' and 'thank you' in Italian now!"

"Teach him French," said Naomi, inspired. "That'll slow him down a bit, and be kind, too. I wish someone had taught me French before I knew any better!"

It proved to be a very good idea. Ruth, equipped with her French dictionary, spent an energetic and educational evening teaching Peter to count 'un, deux, trois', while jumping off the sofa until he was completely breathless, after which they sat down and played Banging Books, a simple game, invented by Peter, during which Ruth opened all his picture books around him and he banged them shut again as loudly and quickly as he could. Ruth could open the books much faster than Peter could shut them, so she always won, but Peter did not seem to mind, and Mrs Collingwood was very grateful, announcing, with apparent satisfaction, that Ruth had obviously worn him out.

98

"How much did you get?" asked Rachel when she returned home.

"Two pounds."

Rachel held a hand out for the coins and Ruth passed them over as meekly as if her little sister had a right to them.

"Naomi said I could look after the money," said Rachel, reaching down the front of her blouse and producing a small jam jar. "I've already put our pocket money in. Much safer than the beastly Post Office!"

"What happens if you lose it?"

"Then Naomi will kill me," said Rachel matter-of-factly, having agreed that part of the arrangement earlier in the day. "Is Peter civilized yet?"

"He's learnt to spit," said Ruth happily.

"Good for you!" said Naomi.

"No, it wasn't me. It's another thing he learnt in Italy. They had to teach him because he kept eating the flowers off the tables."

"You *can* eat pansies and nasturtiums," said Rachel eagerly. "Big Grandma told me one day last summer. Pansies are boring but nasturtiums are hot. You could grow them in those old people's garden and sell them in bunches to vegetarians like Phoebe."

"Don't be daft!"

"I could eat free sample bunches to prove it was possible."

"It would just prove that you would eat anything, everyone knows that anyway."

"And we could give Peter bunches of the wrong sorts, not pansies and nasturtiums and he could spit them out."

"Rachel," said Ruth, "I'm not being horrible and I do think it was brave of you to rob the Post Office, but I think you're crackers. Completely. Nuts. Cracked. Right round the bend."

"Food is food," replied Rachel cheerfully, not at all

distressed to hear these familiar opinions repeated, "and we need money. Everyone knows you starve to death if you don't eat things, that's why they buy food. People pay money for much horribler things than pansies and nasturtiums!"

"School dinners," remarked Phoebe.

"Well, anyway," said Naomi, tired of the pointlessness of the discussion, "we haven't got any pansies or nasturtiums. Or school dinners."

Late in the night Phoebe awoke. A foot had trodden on her legs. A moment later another foot trod on her stomach, there was a thump, scurrying sounds and then a prolonged shaking of the bed as Rachel humped her sledge up on to the top bunk and settled herself down around it. Phoebe knew the symptoms. Rachel was going to try to think and Phoebe closed her eyes and stuffed her head under her pillow in order to go to sleep as quickly as possible before she was called upon to help.

Carefully Rachel tucked her sledge up with rather more than its fair share of the quilt, and then, comforted by its solid presence, began to order her thoughts. Scuffling through her mind she counted them out.

'Money. Food is food. Joseck. Joseck money jam jar!' Yes, there it was, stuffed in a sock, wedged over beside eight of the sixteen books on Africa.

'I really need a double bed,' thought Rachel peevishly and wondered how much they cost. Pounds and pounds probably. Suddenly a whole sentence of a thought came into Rachel's head all at once.

'If I have any money, I spend it on food!'

That was the clue she had been searching for, because not only did she, Rachel, spend her money on food, but so did all her friends. Money burnt holes in their pockets until they had converted it into nourishment and eaten it. All that was necessary in order to become rich, therefore, was to obtain food and sell it to her friends. But Naomi had said they hadn't any, not even pansies or nasturtiums. Not even school dinners. Rachel sighed heavily, curled up into the only shape possible between the books and the sledge, and fell asleep.

"Rachel!"

It was morning and Phoebe was kicking the under-side of her mattress to awaken her.

"Rachel! I've thought of something!"

"Stop kicking."

"Wake up! We've got to get up and make spare packed lunches!"

Rachel sat up, furious that Phoebe had produced so casually the idea she had struggled to grasp all night.

"Spare packed lunches!"

"To sell to people at school," explained Phoebe proudly, "you know, the ones who eat all theirs at playtime and then have to beg for bits of other people's. Like you," she added tactlessly.

There was a long, hurt silence from the top bunk while Rachel considered the advantages and disadvantages of accidentally-on-purpose dropping her sledge on to Phoebe's head and thus silencing her forever.

"Friday is a brilliant day to start," continued Phoebe, unaware of the danger, "because of Mum and Dad both having to be at work for eight o'clock. They never have time to think."

That was true. Friday was the day Mrs Conroy worked the morning shift at the hospital. It was the day of the week that she was least likely to notice any peculiar details of her daughters' behaviour. She would certainly never notice how many lunches they packed themselves in the morning.

"Have you gone back to sleep?" asked Phoebe, craning sideways out of bed to look up at Rachel. "It's a brilliant idea, isn't it? It just came to me all in a flash the second I woke up! But it won't be any good without you," continued Phoebe. "You always make the best packed lunches."

Rachel, who had just balanced her weapon ready for the kill, granted Phoebe a reprieve and pulled it back again. After all, she *did* make the best packed lunches. It really *would* be no good at all without her.

"Come on then," she said, and slithered out of bed.

Luck was with them that Friday morning.

"Fourteen peanut butter and banana sandwiches, ten pence each, one pound-forty," Phoebe counted the takings at the end of the day.

"Three hard-boiled eggs, those ones I found in the back of the fridge," said Rachel, "that's another thirty pence."

"One pound-seventy, then. What about the raisins?"

"Forty pence. Eight handfuls, five pence each, then the packet was empty."

"We ought to charge more for raisins next time. Everybody wanted them. Anyway, that's two pounds-ten. Anything else?"

"That's all," said Rachel, "we ate everything else ourselves. Two pounds-ten is brilliant, though. Ruth and Naomi slave for hours for that much!"

"But we won't tell them yet," said Phoebe.

"No," said Rachel.

The difficulties began on Monday. Many were the complaints when lunch-time came round and Rachel and Phoebe's hungry class-mates, having confidently consumed their own lunches earlier in the day, arrived for further supplies and discovered that they did not exist.

"We didn't say we'd be doing it every day," argued Rachel, chewing up her own packed lunch so fast she nearly choked.

"Just some days," agreed Phoebe.

"Which ones, then?"

"We don't know yet. Fridays probably."

"Not any other day?"

"Depends."

"Well, what are we supposed to do now?"

"Don't know," said Rachel, beginning her apple.

One particularly thin and earnest child tried to reason with them.

"But I ate all my lunch on the way to school. Straight after breakfast, before nine o'clock. It isn't actually possible for me to survive until tea-time. I'll faint."

"You won't," said Phoebe unmoved. "Rachel often eats her lunch on the way to school and she never faints."

"But she's used to it," persisted the Thin One, and went away, unconsoled, even by the free gift of two mints and Rachel's apple core.

"We'll have to try and bring something tomorrow," remarked Phoebe as they walked home that night. "It's a waste of good customers, not having anything to sell them."

"Yes it is," said the Thin One, who was dogging their footsteps, presumably in the hope that they would drop a crust of bread. "I didn't faint but I feel very, very ill and weak!"

"Well, we'll bring something tomorrow," promised Phoebe, thinking that he really did look ill and weak, and trying to remember what he had looked like in the past, before she had starved him.

"Definitely?"

"Definitely," agreed Phoebe, despite her sister's dubious expression.

"We can't really promise," said Rachel as the Thin One left them and staggered feebly through his front gate.

"I'll think of something," said Phoebe cheerfully, and the next morning produced from under her bed a sticky bag of marmalade sandwiches, constructed secretly in the middle of the night.

"They're all modged up," said Rachel, inspecting them critically.

"No one will care," replied Phoebe airily. "Look how hungry they all were yesterday!" The Thin One reinforced her confidence by coming up to her with an anxious expression and informing her that he had eaten his lunch again and she'd better have brought something.

"I have," said Phoebe smugly. However, the Thin One need not have worried. A rival company, the twins from Rachel's class, appeared at lunch-time with chicken paté sandwiches, chocolate biscuits, after dinner mints and a large tin of peaches which they auctioned off to the highest bidder. It went to the Thin One who opened it, cutting himself rather badly in the process, by spiking it on the school railings. This accident did not appear to distress him at all. He consumed peaches and blood with equal gusto and hoped that the twins would be there again tomorrow. Nobody bought any of Phoebe's sandwiches. She stuffed them in the back of her locker and went home, depressed.

"They *did* look all modged up," said Rachel, not entirely sorry to see the collapse of Phoebe's idea.

"*You* needn't talk to me," said Phoebe. "You're a traitor! You bought those twins' sandwiches!"

"Only two!"

"Eating up the profits!"

"They were very good," said Rachel unkindly, "much nicer than squashed marmalade. I wonder what they'll bring tomorrow."

Phoebe had been wondering the same thing, and so, apparently, had quite a few other people. Great disappointment was caused next day when the twins appeared empty-handed, very sheepish, muttering about their mother, and with school dinners booked for them until the end of term. Phoebe triumphantly retrieved her marmalade sandwiches from beneath her gym shoes, and disposed of her entire stock in minutes. The Thin One, who had looked very frightened when the twins' business had failed so abruptly, bought several sandwiches and was almost grovellingly grateful.

"What about tomorrow?" he asked. "Thursday's our day off," said Phoebe loftily, "nothing till Friday now."

"How much did we get today?" asked Rachel that night in bed.

"One pound-twenty, twelve marmalade sandwiches, ten pence each, but that's without the thirty pence you gave to the twins, which makes it ninety pence and two pounds-ten from last Friday. Three pounds altogether."

"It's a lovely way to get rich," murmured Rachel drowsily, and fell asleep planning sandwich fillings for Friday.

"What have you got?"

That was the Thin One, seconds after the dinner bell had rung on Friday lunch-time.

"Crisp and tomato ketchup, peanut butter and tomato ketchup, golden syrup."

The Thin One sighed in delight and bought two of each.

"Sixty pence," said Rachel, who was once again in charge of the money, as well as providing her own brilliant advertising by eating the sandwiches herself as rapidly as possible before they all sold.

"Any chicken paté or chocolate biscuits?" asked someone hopefully.

"Better ask the twins," replied Phoebe.

That Friday was the beginning of Rachel and Phoebe's weeks of glory. Although there were some complaints (the unpredictability of quality caused problems, and not everyone could digest the fillings that Rachel invented from time to time) the service still remained popular. Rival companies, springing up with luxury fillings, tended to be so short-lived that they caused no real competition. 'Conroys' Home-made Spare Packed Lunches' wrote

Rachel in her notebook. (She was collecting recipes in the hope of eventually having them published.)

"Do you think I really ought to call them home-made?" she asked Phoebe.

"Why not?"

"Well, you know where they're made nowadays. I just wondered if the publishers would mind."

"I should think they would mind more if you called them dog kennel-made," replied Phoebe, for recently, in order to avoid questions from their relations, she and Rachel had taken to constructing their wares in Josh's kennel, a large and roomy apartment, easily accessible by climbing over the garden wall. There was plenty of room inside for Rachel, Phoebe, two plates, a loaf of bread, and whatever Rachel had decided should go in the sandwiches that day. Josh obligingly tidied up the crumbs for them afterwards. At first there had been remarks about dog hairs in the fillings, and several clients had disappeared for good, but Rachel and Phoebe had sworn earnestly that they were dog hairs from a very clean dog, and enough customers had remained to keep the business profitable—loyal, good-natured unspoilt people, such as it was a pleasure to cook for, people who would eat anything gratefully, regardless of the fact that it was daily prepared in a dog kennel and stored in a boot locker. It was a happy time for Rachel and Phoebe. They grew very rich and began to talk of going to Africa, as soon as they had time from the sandwich making.

Chapter Seven

"Saturday at last!" said Naomi, reaching over to shake Ruth awake. "Let's go straight to Toby and Emma's."

"What about Peter?"

"What about him?"

"I said we'd stop with him for an hour this morning, while Mrs Collingwood takes Martin to football."

"*We'd* watch him!" exclaimed Naomi. "What a cheek!"

"I help you at Toby and Emma's."

"Toby and Emma are different," said Naomi. "They don't scream. They're house-trained. They don't bite, they don't spit, they don't . . ."

"He'll be in the garden," said Ruth. "Perhaps he'll be better outside. Mr Collingwood's built him a play-pen, huge, with high sides and a door that locks."

"Sounds more like a cage," remarked Naomi.

"It looks like a cage," admitted Ruth frankly, "a very posh one; they designed it specially to fit Peter. They measured his head and how far he could reach, so they knew how far apart to put the bars and how high they had to make it."

"They should have dug a moat round it," said Naomi. "All right, we'll do Toby and Emma this afternoon. What time are they caging up Peter?"

"Ten."

At ten o'clock Peter was lifted into his play-pen. It stood in a sunny corner of the immaculate Collingwood lawn, filled with rugs, bouncy cushions, a rainbow collection of beautiful toys and several teddy bears. At two minutes past ten, Peter was hurling himself at the bars and roaring.

"How strong are they?" Naomi asked Mrs Collingwood apprehensively.

"Very very," replied Mrs Collingwood, leaning over the side to hug Peter. "Very, very strong, my poor baby!" and she yelped as her poor baby sank his teeth into her shoulder.

"I'll be straight back," she promised. "I'm glad there's two of you!"

It took two of them to retrieve the missiles Peter hurled over the side at his departing mother's back. Josh came bouncing up to help too, but departed under a hail of wooden bricks.

"I'm not putting anything hard back in," Naomi told Peter sternly, "you're dangerous! Even Phoebe was never as bad as you!"

"He's not usually this awful," Ruth said. "I think we ought to just leave everything where he throws it and see what he does."

They sat out of range while Peter emptied his play-pen and then proceeded to tear up the lawn with his fists and teeth.

"He's getting awfully dirty," remarked Naomi.

"I know, but he's stopped screaming and they're used to him getting dirty."

"Ruining the grass as well."

"Yes, Mr Collingwood said he would ruin the grass. It's only that one corner."

"He's jolly strong," commented Naomi, looking at the size of the clods Peter was excavating. "What do they feed him on? Dynamite?"

"Martin said he was like that even when he only drank milk. Martin says he's quietened down a lot. He used to scream so loud he could hear him as far as the bus stop. And ringing in his ears all day at school afterwards!"

At that moment a fat black hand shot out from underneath the play-pen.

"He's tunnelling out!" said Naomi in horror.

Ruth jumped to her feet and began picking up toys and putting them back into the play-pen to distract the captive. Peter, looking pleased, plugged up his hole with a plastic telephone and a large yellow duck.

"He just wanted something to play with," said Ruth. "He's being good now. Help me collect everything and we'll put it all back."

Naomi obligingly joined the search for toys. Everything they handed to Peter he accepted with a large grin and piled into his corner. When he had a heap high enough, he clambered on to the top, hauled himself on his stomach on to the top bar and prepared to let himself drop. Ruth caught him just as he crashed to the ground.

"Grazie," said Peter, and kissed her muddily on both cheeks.

"There," said Ruth, flattered. "He was lonely!"

"Yes," agreed Naomi, and added after a moment's thought, "you're going to have to go in with him!"

"In with him? In there?"

"Behind the bars," said Naomi, and went home.

"It's a hard way to earn money," said Ruth. Naomi was washing up the Saturday lunch dishes and Phoebe and Rachel were smashing them, and drying the ones they did not smash. By common consent, Ruth had been allowed to sit and watch.

"What did he do," asked Naomi curiously, "when you got in with him?"

"Nothing much. We played bears for a bit and then he fell asleep all in a heap and then Mrs Collingwood came home."

"Was she cross? What did she say?"

"Why would she be cross?" asked Rachel. "Was Peter all covered in mud too?"

"Worse," said Ruth, "in a way. At least he looked

worse, but I've noticed before that dirt shows up more on Peter than it does on most people."

"More than on Rachel, even?" asked Phoebe, astonished.

"P'raps not," Ruth admitted. "Anyway, all she said was for me to bring my clothes straight round and she'd put them in the washing machine with Peter's before the stains dried in, and she gave me a pound. And tea and chocolate cake and a bottle of posh bubble bath she'd had for a present and she said not to hesitate to borrow her books!"

"Not bad for less than an hour," said Naomi. "What sort of bubble bath?"

"Alpine strawberry and mallow."

"You'll smell like a trifle." Naomi emptied out the washing-up bowl and handed the last mug to Rachel, who dropped it.

"It's a waste to drop them *after* they've been washed," Naomi told her reprovingly. "You should smash them dirty, if you're going to."

"It's only the handle," Rachel inspected the mug, "we can glue it on again. It's been glued before, anyway. Did you know we were coming with you this afternoon?"

"Oh no!" protested Ruth.

"Oh yes," said Mrs Conroy coming in. "Can't leave them alone in the house and I'm going shopping and your father's got to go back in to work. And I've sorted out some seedlings for your garden, Naomi, if you'd like to come and get them."

"Free?" asked Naomi, following her mother to the shed.

"Since when did you hear of me charging old people for a few seedlings?" asked Mrs Conroy. "A nice old couple like that, too; I dropped in for a word with them while you were at your Grandma's. You must be careful not to tire them out. I thought they both looked very frail."

"Ill?" asked Naomi, alarmed.

"Just old," replied her mother, who had looked at Toby and Emma with experienced eyes and decided that if they really wanted a garden and her daughters could do anything to help, then they should do it, and the sooner the better.

It was their first visit to Toby and Emma's since they had arrived home. The garden that Ruth and Naomi had last seen a month ago, bare and wintery and sprouting nothing much but markers to show where they had planted seeds, had grown quite green and bushy in their absence. Someone (Mrs Reed, they later discovered) had cut the grass, but that was all that had been done. Weed and flower seedlings fought for space in the borders, dandelions flowered along the path, and the old apple tree, in full blossom, bent even lower over the garden shed.

"I can't get down to them myself," Toby nodded at the weeds. "You come back just in time! And who are these two young ladies?" he asked, winking at Rachel and Phoebe.

"They're only Rachel and Phoebe," explained Naomi, as she unloaded trays of seedlings and the sixteen library books on Africa from her and Ruth's bicycle baskets. "We've got to look after them while Mum's out shopping. I hope you don't mind."

"The more the merrier," said Toby cheerfully.

"I can dig," Rachel told him.

"You can that, if you've a mind to," agreed Toby. "Is that more books on gardening you've brought?"

"They're books on Africa," said Phoebe. "I needed something to read. You can look at them if you like. Have you ever been?"

"I have," said Toby surprisingly, "fifty-odd years ago! Hot and mucky it was!"

"What were you doing? On holiday?"

"Fighting."

"You shouldn't fight," Rachel told him primly.

"I don't anymore," said Toby. "Now you make yourselves at home while I nip in and fetch Emma. She's been looking forward to you coming all day."

Ruth and Naomi settled down to some much-needed weeding. Phoebe piled the library books into a heap, chose the most interesting, and sat down on the rest to read it. Rachel wandered around the garden, looking for a likely spot to dig for treasure.

Nearly an hour later, Phoebe looked up from her book. Ruth and Naomi had almost met in the middle of the long border. Across the lawn Rachel had found a bare patch.

"A humpy looking bit," thought Rachel hopefully. "Someone must have buried something here a long time ago!"

Someone had buried something there, and not so long ago either. Rachel, industriously scrabbling with her hands, gave a sudden screech of delight and came up with a red feather.

"Rachel!" Ruth and Naomi dashed across the garden.

"There's something under here!" Rachel announced. "Quite big and hard, I can feel the edges! What are you doing?" For her sisters had seized the feather, shoved it back into the hole, and were piling back the earth as quickly as they could, all the while glancing guiltily at the house.

"You idiot!" said Ruth. "Why did you choose that place to dig? That's where they buried Roger!"

Rachel looked suddenly very green and asked if Roger was another old man.

"Roger was their parrot," Naomi said, "and their last gardener got chucked out for digging him up!" Hastily she grabbed the box of geraniums and lobelias her mother had given them and began planting them over Roger's much-disturbed remains.

"I was only looking for treasure," said Rachel, sniffing

her parroty hands and giving them a perfunctory wipe on the grass.

Toby and Emma arrived just in time to hear her. "No harm in looking," said Toby. "Where there's life there's hope!"

"What about where there's dead parrots?" asked Phoebe, but fortunately no one heard her.

"Don't you go digging too deep over there," murmured Emma as she sank into the chair they brought her. "I used to look for treasure when I was your age."

"When you were a Guide?" asked Ruth.

"When I was a girl," said Emma. "I'll just get easy," and there was a pause of silence while Emma's bones and breathing settled into their new surroundings. "When I was a girl," she continued. "You come over here and look at these pictures. These is some of the first Girl Guides!"

Half pitying, half curious, the girls came to look at the bundle of photographs Toby handed to Emma. A party of girls, long-skirted, wearing straw hats, looked back at them.

"Black and white," said Rachel.

"Can you pick me out?" asked Emma.

In silence they stared at the group of round country faces, tanned hands and arms, bright eyes and blowing hair.

"Are they all old ladies now?" asked Rachel, but before Emma could reply, Phoebe had planted a grubby, certain finger on to one of the hats.

"That's you!"

Involuntarily the girls glanced at Emma. More than eighty years had passed since the photograph had been taken, but even that did not seem time enough to wear any of those faces into one so old as Emma's, yet Phoebe said again, quite certainly,

"That's you! Anyone could tell!" and Toby and Emma were nodding in admiration.

★   ★   ★

It was the beginning of a strange understanding between Phoebe and Emma. It was a friendship of equals, both sides seeming oblivious of the eighty-five years that separated them in time. Phoebe made no concession to Emma's obvious frailty. If Emma fell asleep in the middle of a conversation, Phoebe did not hesitate to shake her awake again. She dragged Emma, willy-nilly, through her own convoluted ideas and theories, and when Emma did not understand, Phoebe drew pictures to demonstrate her thoughts, and explained the pictures to Emma. Emma retaliated by ignoring the fact that Phoebe was seven years old, completely poverty stricken, confined to school all day, and hampered by a family who all attempted to bring her up in different directions.

One summer Saturday they sat together in the doorway of the potting shed, under the apple tree, and argued.

"No good blaming other people," said Emma. "What's to stop you going? There's aeroplanes, isn't there? Flying over all the time!" and her head nodded suddenly forwards.

Phoebe glared at Emma and poked her crossly awake.

"You need money. And passports. We'd never be allowed."

"Flying all the time," repeated Emma stubbornly. "There's one now!" and she pointed to a white jet trail crossing the blue midsummer sky.

"Full of rich grown-ups."

"You don't know," murmured Emma. "I shouldn't let it stop me if I wanted to go!"

"Why don't you, then?"

"Don't want to," replied Emma, "garden's full of flowers!" and she fell so deeply asleep that Phoebe got up and marched away.

"Africa!" Emma's voice came scornfully through layers and layers of dreams.

Phoebe, who never told anyone anything, had told her

all about Joseck long ago. Toby knew quite a lot too; he must have heard from Emma. Strangely enough, the girls were not at all worried about this. Secrets seemed safe with Toby and Emma. They were no more likely to talk than the apple tree.

Sometimes Ruth worried about Phoebe's treatment of Emma.

"You shouldn't joggle her like that! It's rude and she's old!"

"It's rude to go to sleep when people are talking to you," pointed out Phoebe. "I don't joggle *hard*. Anyway, she wanted to be awake. She was choosing more people to put in my zoo."

Emma had taken immediately to the idea of Phoebe's zoo, and had more or less enrolled as a sort of under-keeper. Phoebe had constructed a cage for her which she kept in the shed. Lately, Phoebe and Emma had spent a great deal of time together in the shed, looking at library books about Africa and discussing their captives.

"What sort of people does she put in there?" asked Ruth curiously.

"Mostly dead ones," said Phoebe. "She doesn't draw pictures, though. She just writes their names on bits of paper and pushes them through the bars."

Ruth knew better than to comment on this practice, and merely remarked, "Well, don't wear her out, anyway. Come on, it's time to go home; Toby's paid Naomi."

They met Naomi at the garden gate, looking far from happy. It had been very hard to take Toby's money that afternoon, especially as he had also given them chocolate bars and orangeade, a bag of apples and the parrot's old cage, in case they ever got a parrot. In the end, Naomi had settled for half the amount offered.

"What about yon lad in Africa?" Toby had asked, as Naomi dug her hands in her pockets and shook her head.

"We've plenty for him," said Rachel cheerfully, and

patted her stomach so that Toby could hear the jam jar rattle.

"Certain?"

"Oh yes," said Naomi, although far from certain. "Anyway, we only came to look at the garden and to see you. We've done hardly any work."

"You've done more than you know," said Toby. "Ay well, we'll settle up one day."

"What about Joseck, though?" asked Ruth as they walked home. "We've only got six pounds and it ought to be posted by the weekend."

Rachel and Phoebe glanced smugly at each other, and later that evening produced ten pounds in silver and coppers.

"We earned it," said Phoebe casually.

"How?" demanded Naomi, and when they would not say, she glared very hard at Rachel and asked, "Legally?"

"Oh yes!" said Rachel and Phoebe together, who honestly believed that it was legal to manufacture sandwiches out of stolen property in a dog kennel and then sell them to school children.

Ruth took the money very doubtfully, and purchased a ten pound postal order with some trepidation, although she could hardly believe that Rachel would have found the courage to rob the Post Office twice. It appeared that she had not; nothing happened when she went in, except that Rachel's cashier threw his hands up into the air and shouted that he surrendered, but then he did that every time a Conroy girl entered the door, it was not unusual. Rachel's sisters were beginning to be extremely tired of the joke, but felt in no position to complain.

"We do need another way of getting money, though," Naomi remarked that night.

"I know, I'm trying to think of one."

Ruth fell asleep still trying, and it was not until her

116

end-of-term class trip to London that inspiration finally arrived. She came home exhausted, dirty, and glowing.

"Artists were drawing pictures, just in the streets," she told Naomi, "and people were giving them money! Paying!"

"*In* the streets?" asked Naomi, going cold with dread.

"*On* the streets," said Ruth, "on the paving stones! Chalks and pastels mostly. People stopped to look and put money in their tins or hats or chalk boxes!"

"Oh no!" said Naomi in horror. "Anyway, it's begging!"

"'Course it isn't!"

"I bet it's against the law."

"They were doing it in London," said Ruth fanatically, "policemen everywhere. It can't be."

"Anyway, I can't draw."

"I can. And you could colour in."

"I won't."

"Some of the pictures were rubbish. People still paid."

"It's a terrible idea. It's worse than robbing the Post Office. Someone might see us! Anything!"

"People are *meant* to see," said Ruth, and Naomi recognized a familiar note of madness in her voice. Ruth, usually the sanest of them all, occasionally flipped. At such times she was not to be reasoned with; the only thing to do was to wait until the phase was over and then deal as best as possible with the consequences.

"I'm not colouring in," said Naomi. "I'm not doing anything to help. I'm not coming near you. I think you're mad. And you can do it in disguise, so that no one knows you're my sister!"

"Will you help me with the disguise?"

"All right," said Naomi begrudgingly.

For the first time in her life, Naomi prayed for rain. She prayed that it would rain all summer, from the first day of the summer holidays to the last, excluding the two weeks they were to spend in Cumbria with Big Grandma. During the first week of the holidays, it seemed that her prayers were to be answered. It poured and poured; the pavements streamed with water, it was the sort of weather to make any hopeful street artist search for an alternative career, but Naomi was disturbed to see that Ruth's ambitions remained undampened by the deluge.

"It will wash the pavements clean," she remarked, and went out into the down-pour to locate a suitable site for her efforts. Naomi refused to go with her and told Ruth quite frankly that she hoped she caught pneumonia, but Ruth returned home triumphant.

"There's a beautiful patch of clean paving stones right outside the church," she announced. "Just right, and miles away from the market and you know that's where all the policemen lurk about. We'll be quite safe."

"What d'you mean 'we'?" demanded Naomi. "You needn't think I'll be there, because I won't."

"I think I'd better start practising pictures," said Ruth.

"Where?"

"Guard the door!" Ruth began pulling up the tacks that held their bedroom carpet and rolling it back.

"You are crazy," said Naomi, but nevertheless she guarded the door while Ruth drew the local church, Van Gogh's 'Sunflowers' and Tigger from *Winnie the Pooh* on the bedroom floor-boards.

"Look at all the chalk you're using up!"

"I bought stacks," replied Ruth. "I spent all my pocket and Peter money."

"What an awful waste!"

Ruth did not bother to argue. The next day she rubbed out the sunflowers, church and Tigger, and drew a beautiful parrot and the Prime Minister's head and shoulders in black and white.

"Isn't it cheating to copy out of newspapers?" asked Naomi.

"They were doing it in London," replied Ruth, not looking up and printing 'COUNTRY CRASHES!' very neatly under the picture of the Prime Minister.

"What'll you do if it rains all summer?" asked Naomi.

"The weather forecast says it'll be dry by the end of the week."

Naomi looked very depressed and went on a mysterious trip to Toby and Emma's. She returned with a bulging carrier bag of old clothes.

"What's that?"

"Disguise," said Naomi briefly.

A long letter from Joseck arrived. He wrote that he was well and very happy to have four friends in England. He told them that when he took their letter home, there was his mother, cooking beans and bread for supper, just like Ruth. He had read the letter to his family and his mother had laughed and said she did not burn the bread and his father said tell your friend Rachel that his friend saw two lions cross the road only a few evenings ago, and that Mari was the daughter of his mother's friend, and was, even as he wrote, sitting on her hands refusing to do anything. She had drawn her lady a picture of rain and now she said her hands hurt and she could not write . . . He wrote that from the school window he could see the bus from Nairobi coming along the road and that it had stopped outside the school and four people climbed out and Joseck had a thought that it might be his friends from England, although he knew all the time that really it was not.

"One day it might be, though," said Rachel when they came to this part of the letter.

Naomi sighed. Ten pounds a month were hard enough to find, never mind air fares to Nairobi.

"Have you and Phoebe any more money?" she asked. "We'll need to send another ten pounds before we go to Big Grandma's."

119

Rachel and Phoebe shook their heads. The Home-made Spare Packed Lunch business had been temporarily closed when term ended.

"Ruth's going to get some," said Phoebe. "She told me she's found an easy way!"

"Easy!" snorted Naomi.

"Easier than looking after Peter, I think she meant. She wouldn't tell us what it was, though."

Rachel remarked that she hated secrets and that she wished she knew what Ruth was planning and Naomi thought privately that Rachel was lucky. She wished she did not know, and she wished it even more the next morning when Ruth's bed was found empty but unmade and Ruth herself could not be discovered anywhere.

"Well at least she had something to eat before she went out," Mrs Conroy said, and she looked crossly at the crumbs all over the breadboard, the jammy butter and the bottle of spilt milk.

"Perhaps she got hungry in the night," suggested Rachel, but Mrs Conroy said no, that was the morning's milk spilt all over the table. Certain clothes, an enormous straw hat and a greenish-greyish old mac of Emma's had disappeared from Naomi's supply of disguises. Naomi noted this fact with mingled horror and relief and told herself that it was none of her business.

Outside the church, in the early morning sunshine, the Owl and the Pussy Cat, Hey Diddle Diddle, the Prime Minister, a stained glass window and Van Gogh's 'Sunflowers' already brightened the paving stones. A small shabby figure rested contentedly beside these glories, eating chalk, jam sandwiches and dirt in about equal quantities. Beside her, also eating a jam sandwich, stood the lanky figure of the vicar. He was admiring the design of the stained glass window.

"It's the animals in the ark," explained Ruth. "I thought

I'd do something religious because of the church."

"Please don't get into trouble," said the vicar.

"I've got old clothes on," said Ruth cheerfully.

"I didn't mean that . . . Well, I shall be in and out of the church. Come and find me if you need to. Really I shouldn't encourage you, but good luck," and the vicar dropped fifty pence on to the tigers in the ark and disappeared into the church.

For some time Ruth earned no more. People passing by the church on their way to the market square stopped to admire the pictures and to exclaim at the state of the artist's hands, but no one seemed to think they ought to pay for the privilege. After a while Ruth realized why, and soon a steady trickle of money found its way from the straw hat to her jeans' pocket. A small scruffy man in an old-fashioned hat and sunglasses walked very close to her, dropped a penny on to the picture of the cow jumping over the moon, and hissed,

"Put your hat on!"

He had such a familiar voice that Ruth looked up.

"Put your hat on!"

The little old man shuffled off, sat down on the church-yard wall and glared at Ruth. Despite the heat of the day, he wore a long overcoat and a scarf wound round his face, almost to his eyes. Wellington boots came up to the hem of his coat. Ruth was so sure that she knew who he was, that she left her pictures and sat down on the wall beside him. Immediately he leapt to his feet and hurried away.

At that moment a fat woman walked straight across the Prime Minister's face, said, "Sorry duck!" and dropped twenty pence into the straw hat.

The vicar came out and asked, "Everything all right? No trouble from anyone?" and by the time Ruth had retrieved her money and assured him that everything was fine, the little man from the church wall had gone away.

It seemed he had not gone far, however; he reappeared

half an hour later and dropped half a bar of nut chocolate on the man in the moon. Stuck into the wrapper was a note. 'Put your hat on. And your coat. Egg Yolk Wendy and Gavin coming this way. What about dinner?'

"Naomi!" exclaimed Ruth and the little man nearly jumped out of his skin.

"Don't shout my name! And you're supposed to be in disguise! And rub that out!" Naomi pointed a wellington boot to where her sister had signed her name across the paving stones.

"Do you think it's too vain?" asked Ruth earnestly, and found she was suddenly talking to empty space. Naomi had leapt nimbly over the churchyard wall and been replaced by a very familiar push-chair.

"Good dog!" said a loud and friendly voice.

"Bad news!" announced Mrs Collingwood cheerfully. "Awfully sorry but you're breaking the law, Ruth! Policeman approaching from the right! Vicar approaching from the church, peculiar little man hovering in the background! Time to stop, I'm afraid."

Her voice was like sudden cold water on Ruth's dreaming head. All at once she awoke from the week's madness and saw the pavement of pictures, the policeman from the market threading his way towards her, the vicar hesitating on the path, and Mrs Collingwood's face. It bore the expression of exasperated cheerfulness that she usually reserved for late-night telephone calls from the police station. Ruth also noticed that Mrs Collingwood had thoughtfully parked Peter on the greater part of her signature, and was busy scuffing out the end she was standing on.

"Awfully silly to sign your name," she remarked.

"That's what I said!" Naomi, hat even lower and scarf even higher, suddenly reappeared between them. "Give me your money! Stuff it in this bag!"

"Good gracious!" said Mrs Collingwood.

122

"Quick, before that policeman gets here!"

It was almost too late. Even as Ruth transferred the last handful of change to the little man's bag, the policeman arrived beside her. Hastily the little man jumped the churchyard wall, dodged the vicar and sprinted across the gravestones. As he ran, he shed his hat and scarf, dropped his glasses and abandoned his coat. Before he was out of sight, he had transformed into Naomi, hurrying across the market place in wellington boots.

"That someone you know?" asked the policeman.

"Yes," said Ruth.

Mrs Collingwood, to cheer Ruth up, informed her that she was the dirtiest person ever to enter her bath-tub.

"Impressive, you've got to admit," she said, "when you think of my husband after rugby, or Martin after football, or Peter!"

Ruth looked completely uncheered.

"Well, we can't go and talk to your mother with you looking like that! You know I had to promise I'd mention it to her. It all looked so odd; not just the pictures, but Naomi's clothes, and her running off like she did and the silly old vicar, offering to witness you'd been robbed!"

"S'pose he was only trying to help."

"Lucky the policeman recognized me, and that poor old Peter was sick when he was! I wish I'd noticed him with that chalk. It may have been non-toxic, but it was a very nasty shade of blue!"

"Sorry."

"I shall play it down to your mother," said Mrs Collingwood reassuringly. "Don't look so upset!"

Play it down as she might, Mrs Collingwood could not hide the fact that Ruth had been discovered drawing pictures in the street for money and had been ordered to desist from this rash enterprise by . . .

"A very pleasant man," said Mrs Collingwood. "I've dealt with him before. Very practical! A charming . . ."

"Policeman," finished Mrs Conroy, who knew too well the pleasant practical men her neighbour usually dealt with. She was very angry with Ruth.

"So did she do it?" Rachel asked cheerfully that night.

"Who do what?"

"Ruth. Get that easy money for Joseck?"

There was a long silence while Naomi considered the day and Rachel gazed at her expectantly.

"Well, she got it," said Naomi eventually, "but it wasn't easy."

Chapter Eight

The week before they were due to depart for Cumbria, the weather turned damp and dismal and the Conroy house seemed even smaller than usual. Smaller and full of suspicious glances. Mrs Conroy was keeping a close eye on her daughters, and no sooner did they disappear into their bedrooms in furtive twos and threes, than she routed them out again and found them jobs to do. Their reply to Joseck's letter was written in Toby and Emma's potting shed, the only private place they could find.

"Please ask," said Rachel, "about snakes. I cannot stop thinking about them, ever since I read that book. I dreamt they were in bed last night but it turned out to be my sledge rope. Getting round my legs. I kicked it out but I still keep feeling them."

"You needn't have kicked it out so hard," said Phoebe bitterly. "It hurt!"

"Some snakes," said Rachel, "swallow goats by twisting round their legs and squashing 'em flat. That's what I thought it was. And I can't stop wondering," she finished, "if I am bigger than a goat, or smaller, or the same size! Roughly. Ask Joseck!"

"He will think you're mad," said Naomi, who was doing the writing. "Still, he would be right," and she wrote,

> *Rachel has read that some African snakes eat goats, and now she is worried. She does not know if she came to Africa and met one of those snakes and it swallowed her, would she be the right size.*

Of course we know we couldn't really, continued
Naomi, *but when you wrote about the bus from Nairobi
we asked about air fares at the travel shop. Only for
thinking about. It would cost a lot of money.*

Emma appeared in the shed doorway at that moment.

"Saw you was here," she remarked, sinking down on
to the garden chair Ruth pushed towards her.

"Do you mind?"

"Why should I? What you doing?"

"Writing to Joseck in Africa."

"Have you told him you'll be along one day?"

"We found out how much it costs; hundreds of pounds
to fly from London."

"This ain't London," said Emma, as if where they were
at the moment was much closer.

"We'd have to go to London, though."

"You'd go half price," said Emma, dismissing that
problem.

"And there's snakes," said Rachel gloomily, "big
enough to swallow goats, even if we got there!"

"Scared of snakes?" asked Emma, sounding surprised
and shoving a new piece of paper through the bars of her
zoo.

"Everyone is."

"Not me," contradicted Emma. "I've never been scared
of nothing. You put that in for me! Me hands are shaking!"

Ruth took the slip of paper, and read, in Emma's shaking writing, the Prime Minister's name.

"Getting crowded," she commented as she pushed it
through the bars.

"Their problem," said Emma. "Anyway, I'm getting
back. That was all I come for. You say hello to that boy
in Africa for me."

"I'm sorry," Naomi inspected the envelope. "I would
but I've just licked it up and it's stuck. We will next time."

126

"Say it when you get there," said Emma, "if them snakes don't scare you off!" and she wandered back to the house.

"Why does she always make it sound so easy?" asked Naomi rather crossly, "when she must know it's practically impossible even to get the ten pounds every month!"

"Mum's awfully mad with Ruth," remarked Rachel dispassionately.

"She's mad with all of us. She hasn't got over you robbing the Post Office yet, or Phoebe smashing her train. It's not just me. I think we ought to try and not show up very much for a while."

"What do you mean?"

"Just be there," said Ruth, "but not do anything that anyone would notice."

"Slope around," Naomi said.

"Unsuspiciously," agreed Ruth.

"Not do anything?" asked Rachel, "that's easy!"

For a day or two they did not do anything and it *was* easy. Home grew peaceful and Mrs Conroy appeared to relax. It lasted until two days before they were to set off to Cumbria, and was spoilt by the Thin One, who appeared on the front doorstep, rang the bell, and asked Mrs Conroy if Rachel and Phoebe would still be doing it in the holidays.

"Because I think it would be a good thing," he explained earnestly. "People still get hungry! Even those marmalade ones would do if they did. I came to ask, in case they were and I hadn't heard."

"What do you mean?" asked Mrs Conroy.

"I've been away," explained the Thin One, "on holiday, so I might not have heard."

"Heard what?"

"If Rachel and Phoebe still do them in the holidays. I don't see why they shouldn't. I know some people thought they ought to stop but I never did. They said it was a clean dog and it is, I've seen it. It's that one, isn't it?" and he pointed to Josh, who was enjoying the sun in the Collingwood front garden and looking, as the Thin One truly remarked, beautifully clean.

"Tell me," said Mrs Conroy, "exactly what you are talking about. As if I were a very stupid person."

"Are Rachel and Phoebe still selling those home-made spare packed lunches?" the Thin One asked, as plainly as he could. "The ones they used to make in that dog's kennel last term?"

"So much," said Naomi sarcastically, "for keeping a low profile and sloping around and not doing anything to be noticed!"

"Yes," said Ruth.

"There's only me with any sense," continued Naomi, conveniently forgetting that less than a week before, she had paraded through the market place dressed as an old man and had, thus disguised, robbed a street artist in front of a policeman, a solicitor and a vicar.

Ruth pointed this out to her, and Naomi said it did not count because their mother had not found out.

"Only because Mrs Collingwood didn't tell on you like she did on me," said Ruth, "anyway, arguing doesn't help."

They had sat together on the stairs and listened to the snivelling sounds that came from their little sisters' bedroom. Rachel and Phoebe had been cross-questioned and spanked, not particularly ferociously, because in her heart of hearts Mrs Conroy did not think spanking did any good, but hard enough to relieve her outraged feelings and upset their dignity.

"And you two can come down!" called Mrs Conroy up the stairs: "Goodness knows, they need no encouragement from you! Do you realize what might have happened if anyone had fallen ill? Your father and I might have ended

128

up in court! I've taken the money off them they said they'd made; what's left of it anyway. Six or seven pounds and apparently they've spent another ten on heaven knows what, sweets and rubbish I suppose . . ."

Ruth and Naomi cringed into opposite corners of the sofa.

"You'd think they weren't fed at home! First one thing and then another! The money that's left will have to go to charity, I suppose. I couldn't begin to try and give it back . . . I've told them if I hear one word about any sort of trouble at your grandma's, none of you will be trusted to go there again. And the same goes for you two! Street artist indeed! I haven't forgotten!"

"They *were* doing it in London," Ruth argued. "No one minded there. It looked good fun!"

"Begging!" said Mrs Conroy. "And that reminds me, you can bring down any money you got and it's going to charity, too!"

"There wasn't any," said Ruth, "not by the time I'd bought the chalks, and then someone grabbed some of it."

"I'm writing to your grandmother," said Mrs Conroy, not noticing Naomi's alarmed expression, "and warning her about everything that's happened this year, and if anything goes wrong, you'll be home on the next train!"

"What's worrying you?" asked Big Grandma. "Have you been worrying non-stop since Easter, or does it come in fits and starts? What have you all been up to? Strange tales have arrived from your mother! Is there anything you'd feel better telling me about?"

The long journey to Cumbria was over, the celebration tea was eaten, Graham, their friend of the previous summer, had departed for home. They sat together on the front steps of Big Grandma's house and watched the sun slide down towards the sparkling sea.

"Are you in trouble with the law?" asked Big Grandma cheerfully.

"Not now," said Rachel, remembering with horror her run from the Post Office. No one else replied, so Big Grandma said no more until Ruth asked, as casually as she knew how, what people did to earn money in Cumbria.

"Farm mostly," said Big Grandma, "and tourism further inland, of course."

"I meant children," said Ruth.

"What sort of money are we talking about?" asked Big Grandma. "Hundreds or thousands? Pounds or pence?"

"Ten pounds!" All four spoke at once and far too quickly.

The sun flamed brighter and brighter and Big Grandma, watching it, remarked, "In Africa the sun sets at six o'clock every night! Did you know that?"

"Yes," said Naomi, so abruptly that Big Grandma glanced sharply at her.

"Of course, it will do on the equator," Big Grandma agreed, "obvious when you think about it, but I was astonished when I realized it myself. Everything still all right in Africa, Phoebe?"

"It'll be nice," said Phoebe, after the shocked silence that followed this question, "not to have to sleep in the bottom bunk, with Rachel and her sledge in the top one waiting to fall out."

"You're always being horrible about my sledge," said Rachel.

"Did you think of bringing it with you?" Big Grandma asked her politely, and Rachel replied that she had, and had in fact packed it in its sledge case in readiness, and had been quite prepared to carry it herself, but when she unloaded it at the station it had been taken from her by her mother.

"I'd polished it ready to come," she said sadly.

"Life is tough," said Big Grandma.

★   ★   ★

Ten pounds!

Big Grandma's granddaughters were in bed, and Big Grandma was thinking hard. Ten pounds was the amount she had given them each at Christmas, and the sum that Rachel had extracted in so reckless a manner from the Post Office. Ten pounds had been the amount Mrs Conroy had not been able to account for, from the funds of the Spare Packed Lunch Company. It seemed highly probable that ten pounds had been the amount that Ruth gained and lost in her brief career as a street artist, and it was more than likely that Ruth's Peter-sitting, and Naomi's gardening were done in order to obtain more ten pound sums.

Big Grandma's brain fitted together further pieces of the jigsaw.

Strange that they were still obsessed with Africa. Big Grandma, helping with the unpacking that evening, had noticed that their holiday reading consisted of nothing but books on the continent. All these things, unconnected, had meant nothing reasonable to Mrs Conroy, but to Big Grandma, thoughtfully regarding Phoebe's sketch of the money inside her train through the slit, they were beginning to form a picture.

'Ten pounds again,' thought Big Grandma, 'and obtained with disastrous results to the train!' Carefully she laid Phoebe's picture back down in the drawer of her desk kept for letters from her grandchildren.

Africa! From another drawer she took a small pile of blue airmail letters; drawings by an African child of a little girl, a man with eyes like stones, and a picture of rain.

"Extra pocket money! Holiday money! Call it what you like!" Big Grandma laid a ten pound note on the breakfast table. "If it's the cost of a peaceful holiday it's cheap at the price!"

"Thank you!" said Ruth and Naomi together, amazed.

Big Grandma was smiling at her granddaughters as if

she was fond of them, and although they realized that of course she *did* like them, she usually managed to conceal it so well that such a manifestation was quite startling.

"Make it last," said Big Grandma.

"It'll last us right till the end of September," said Rachel and promptly doubled up with pain as three people kicked her shins under the table.

"Pigs!" said Rachel. "Anyway, give it to me!" Reaching down into the stomach region of her sweat-shirt she produced her jam jar, banked the money and stuffed it out of sight.

"Are you rich?" Phoebe asked Big Grandma. "Where do you get it from?"

"Get what from?"

"Money. That ten pound note."

"That particular one came from the Post Office," said Big Grandma, grinning at Rachel, "an institution which I hear you no longer patronize! Surely that jam jar is very uncomfortable, Rachel?"

"Yes, very," said Rachel, "especially running."

"Years since I ran anywhere," mused Big Grandma, "probably couldn't anymore."

"How would you escape, then?" asked Rachel, "if you were chased, say, by one of those huge snakes that swallow goats?"

"Rachel," explained Ruth, "is obsessed with snakes that swallow goats."

"Vain I am not," said Big Grandma cheerfully, "but I flatter myself that neither in face nor figure do I resemble a goat! You people worry too much! Stop it until September! Get outside and enjoy yourselves!"

In the middle of August the end of September seemed an age away. It was six weeks until they need start panicking about the October instalment of Joseck's money. Nothing happened to spoil that holiday; nothing bad enough to be reported to Mrs Conroy, anyway. Ruth, acting on information obtained from their holiday reading, cooked fried eggs over a bonfire of dampish cowpats and temporarily prostrated them all, which was not her fault at all. Some people used nothing else.

"They must do," said Naomi, "or they'd die."

"They don't."

"Well, they must use them drier."

"The fumes," said Phoebe, "tasted worse than the eggs."

"Can't be properly vegetarian," remarked Naomi, "eating cowpat fumes!"

Even Rachel had not enjoyed her lunch, and had cruelly pointed out to Ruth that nothing she had ever eaten in her whole life ("and I've eaten all sorts") had caused her to be so sick.

Naomi discovered a pair of ancient sheep shears, and aided by Graham, who should have known better, sheared half of one of Graham's mother's pet lambs. The lamb, which had become quite a large sheep, escaped and took refuge in Graham's mother's kitchen.

"Thought you said it was a pet one," said Naomi.

"It is, that's why it ran into the kitchen."

"You didn't house-train it very well."

Graham's mother, who had equipped Graham with a shovel and Naomi with a mop, explained that one could not house-train sheep, and Naomi, mopping round the cooker, privately thought that if that was the case it was silly to keep them as pets, but she did not say so. She was very fond of Graham's mother.

"Lucky you have tiles and not a carpet," she remarked as she sloshed busily around her hostess's feet, and Graham's mother agreed that it was.

Rachel did nothing alarming at all; she ate a great deal, and what she could not manage during the day she took to bed and ate at night, but that was her own affair. She slept just as comfortably among the crumbs and egg shells and apple cores as she did in her own bed at home. Phoebe, however, managed to fulfil a long-held ambition, starting Big Grandma's car and driving it unhurriedly into the forsythia bush. Fortunately, she neglected to take the handbrake off, so it moved very slowly and no great damage was done. Big Grandma, although voicing her opinions very forcefully on all these occasions, gallantly forbore to relate them to Mrs Conroy, and they left for home with their reputations intact.

"How are you?" Graham's mother asked Big Grandma, meeting her the day after the girls had departed.

"Bloody but unbowed," said Big Grandma. "Missing them, I'm afraid!"

Back at home, they missed Big Grandma. Despite her toughness and her sometimes unflatteringly honest opinions, she had seemed to be somehow on their side.

"On the very first morning she gave us ten pounds!" Naomi told Toby and Emma.

"For yon lad in Africa?" asked Toby.

"She doesn't know anything about him."

"Bet she does," said Emma.

"Emma," said Phoebe, remembering the conversation that first breakfast time in Cumbria, "can you run?"

"Run where?"

"Anywhere?"

"Dare say. If I wanted to."

"Go on, then."

"Don't want to, do I? Why should I?"

"What if you wanted to run away from something?"

"I'm no coward," said Emma, "I told you that before!"

134

"No, and never was," agreed Toby, watching Emma's head drop sleepily forwards, "and neither you be, either! You never get anywhere worth going by running away!"

"We don't run away!"

"You grab your chances," said Toby. "Like I did, when you come to see my garden. It's been a picture all summer!"

"Good," said Rachel, who beyond digging up Roger, had done nothing at all to contribute to the brightness of Toby's garden.

"What's the plan for this afternoon, then?" he asked. "We've a dozen cream buns wants eating when you're hungry. Should you like them now?"

"Big Grandma said if we cut the dead heads off things like cornflowers and stuff, they'd all flower again, so we thought we'd do that."

"I'm going to dig for treasure," Rachel told him. "I haven't for ages."

"Well, I can't say we've buried any since you last looked," Toby remarked, "however, no harm in trying. You're in the wrong spot altogether though; you want to be down by the marshes. That's where I used to look when I was a boy."

"Why, what's down by the marshes?"

"King John's treasure," Emma woke up as suddenly as she had fallen asleep. "Have you never heard tell of that?"

They shook their heads.

"Every child in the district looked for King John's treasure in my day," said Toby. "King John, bad lot by all accounts, run off with the crown jewels and money and gold and goodness knows what. Dropped the lot crossing the marshes, that's history, that is, you should have learned it at school."

"Why was he crossing the marshes?"

"To escape," said Toby, "though I don't recall what."

"Why didn't he stop and pick it up again?"

"That's what I used to ask," said Emma.

"How d'you know it's still there?"

"Because no one ever found it," answered Toby reasonably.

"Be all muddy now, and rusty."

"Jewels'll wash," said Emma, "and gold don't rust; that's what I used to think."

Even Rachel was rather sceptical about the possibility of gold and money and the crown jewels lying round waiting to be found by some lucky schoolchild.

"How long ago was it?" she asked, "because Ruth saw the crown jewels on her school trip to London before the end of term. Somebody must have found them and given them back."

"There couldn't be two lots," agreed Ruth doubtfully.

"I bet he picked them up again," said Phoebe, "even a really stuck-up king would bend down and pick them up again if he dropped the crown jewels! Even I would!"

"You're not a king," Naomi pointed out.

"That proves it then," said Phoebe dismissively. "If I'd do it when they weren't even my jewels, then King John would definitely . . . there's Mrs Reed."

Mrs Reed paused at the fence to admire the bright patchwork flower-beds, and called out, "Bless you!" as she passed.

"Why'd she say that?" asked Naomi and Emma suspiciously.

"Oh, she says that every morning," explained Phoebe, "after school assembly, after she's read the bans. Last term she banned chewing gum, bubble gum, grass fights, running in the corridor, screaming competitions, talking Australian and my collection of ants I was taming in my desk. I expect she's just practising for school next week."

"All them rules," said Emma scathingly. "You don't want to take no notice!"

"We don't," said Phoebe reassuringly.

Chapter Nine

In the second week of September, school began again. The day before the beginning of term, Martin-the-good came round and formally announced that he would no longer be holding up the school bus for them in the mornings.

"But that means we'll miss it nearly every day!" said Ruth astonished, and Martin said he was afraid that was the case and he hoped they would not take it personally.

"What shall we do about waiting for the post?" Ruth asked Naomi. "Letters from Joseck might arrive any day!"

"We won't do anything," replied Naomi calmly, "and Martin will hold up the bus for us just the same as usual. You wait and see!" They were deliberately late the next morning, and sure enough, there was Martin, one foot on the kerb and the other on the bus, vowing he would never do it again.

"It shouldn't be allowed!" Egg Yolk Wendy broke off a detailed description of her summer to complain. "Did you know I've just been back from Europe?"

"No," said Ruth shortly.

"Seven countries," said Wendy, "in two weeks! Eight counting England! Didn't Gavin tell you? I sent him a postcard and told him to pass it on."

"Forgot," mumbled Gavin. For once he was sitting on his own, Wendy's new sports equipment requiring all of the spare seat beside her.

"France I was sick," said Wendy, jabbing across the aisle at Gavin's foot with her new hockey stick, "Switzerland, we bought four cuckoo clocks, Italy all right except for the mountains and horrible toilets, Austria quite liked,

Luxembourg we just drove through, Dad said it wasn't worth stopping, Belgium really boring, then we had to go back to France though we'd seen it once already . . .''

Just to annoy her, Naomi moved and sat next to Gavin. Wendy tossed her egg-yolk yellow pony-tail and said Naomi could if she liked because she was thinking of finishing with him and Gavin looked hopeful for the first time for months, but then grew gloomy again as Wendy added she intended to keep him for a friend.

"Who are you going to have instead?" enquired Ruth, and Wendy replied that she did not know, but she was wondering about Martin who was so much more mature (and rich) than Gavin. Martin laughed good-naturedly and said he would rather die and Gavin said, "Oh please Martin!" At which exchange of remarks, Wendy took offence and said she hated boys and was going in for women's lib.

"You'll be able to do what you like now on Saturdays," Naomi said to Gavin.

"Will I?"

"'Course you will! Didn't you hear? You won't have to go trailing round town after Wendy!"

"Won't I?"

"You've been dumped! She's going in for women's lib!"

"What can I do, then?"

"What did you use to do?"

It was so long since Gavin had done anything of his own free will, unorganized by Wendy, that it took him some time to remember.

"I used to go bird-watching down the marshes!" he announced, and was astonished to see Naomi's face brighten with interest.

Ever since their return from Cumbria, Naomi had been wondering about the next ten pounds. Rather than bear any more of her sisters' far too public and embarrassing ways of getting money, she had resolved to get it herself. Having come so far in her decision-making, Naomi stuck. Try as she might, she could think of no discreet and respectable way of making ten pounds. Gone were the days when she could bear to charge Toby and Emma for the work she did in their garden, and she had almost decided to choose the least-valued of her books and dispose of them in the town's second-hand book shop, when Gavin recalled his past life of freedom and awoke Naomi's imagination.

What if she were to find King John's treasure?

Her sisters, she knew, did not believe in it. Naomi had mentioned the subject again, and Phoebe had repeated her argument that anyone who dropped the crown jewels would certainly pick them up again. Rachel had agreed, and said they obviously had done, since Ruth had seen them in London only a few months before. Ruth had gone so far as to look King John up in the library encyclopaedia and had found no reference to lost jewels, or gold, or flights across the Lincolnshire marshes. On the other hand, Toby and Emma had been completely unmoved by what Emma called 'book talk' and had remarked that whoever wrote the encyclopaedia obviously was not a local chap.

"How do you know?" Ruth had asked, and Emma had replied that of course he wasn't, otherwise he would have put in about King John losing his treasure down by the marshes.

Anyway, Naomi decided, it was worth a try, and she asked Gavin, "How did you get there?"

"Where?"

"Marshes."

"On my bike," said Gavin.

"Are you going on Saturday, then? Now Wendy's dumped you?"

"I only said I thought I would," interrupted Wendy.

"Too late!" Ruth, Naomi, Martin and several other

people who had pitied Gavin for months, all spoke together.

"I might have," said Gavin, uncomplainingly accepting the majority decision on his love life, "but Dad's sold my bike."

"You can borrow Ruth's," said Naomi immediately, "if you'll show me the way."

"Why?" asked Gavin alarmed, and added bravely that he didn't want any more girlfriends yet.

"No, no, no!" said Naomi through gritted teeth, "I just want to go there, that's all."

"You can't have got over me yet," Wendy reminded Gavin, and Gavin meekly agreed that he hadn't.

"Good luck!" said Ruth the following Saturday. "Hope it doesn't rain; it looks a bit grey! Don't let Gavin wreck my bike! I don't know how you got him to agree to go."

"I didn't really," admitted Naomi. "In the end I just told him he was going and I was coming with him. I think he likes that better than having to make his mind up!"

It seemed Naomi was right. At every crossroads on the bike ride to the marshes, Gavin paused and asked Naomi which way she thought they ought to take, and each time Naomi replied with diminishing patience that she did not know and ordered Gavin to go the way he had always done in the past, and Gavin, following these instructions, finally brought them to their destination. With great relief Naomi abandoned him on a muddy patch of reeds and after impressing on him that he was not to go back without her, departed to look for gold.

The marsh was immense. It stretched out to the left as far as Naomi could see, and curved round to the right for miles. Far out on the horizon a silver line that was the sea marked the outward boundary. Naomi climbed a stile and squinted out into the late September afternoon. Nothing Toby or Emma had said had indicated the size of the place.

She had imagined a large muddy field, and instead it was like finding another country.

"King John might have dropped them anywhere," she said. "The fool!"

Pointless even to get down from the stile. Naomi, hunched down against the cold sea wind, stared out into the greyness and searched for a glimpse of gold and at that moment the sun broke through the clouds.

Immediately the landscape was transformed. The munching brown cattle suddenly gleamed like golden beasts on an old tapestry and the bleached summer grasses acquired a blond rinse. Every puddle and pond and creek, right out to the glimmering horizon, became a sheet of mirrored gold. The crown jewels, stacked in a heap in the middle would have been impossible to pick out, and Naomi knew it. Eventually, stiff and chilled from sitting too long, she clambered down from the stile and went in search of Gavin. There he was, still parked beside his patch of reeds. He waved cheerfully as Naomi approached and pointed to a flock of birds that rose between them.

"What?" asked Naomi.

"Golden plover!" said Gavin.

Ruth was waiting at the gate when the treasure-hunters arrived home. The first thing she saw was Gavin's sad clown's face beaming with satisfaction and her heart gave a sudden bump of hope.

"Any luck?" she asked.

"Brilliant!" replied Gavin, causing her expectations to rise even higher, only to fall once again at the sight of Naomi. No hint of treasure sparkled in her sister's eyes. Her bike basket was perfectly empty, and her pockets completely flat.

"Didn't you find anything, then?" Ruth asked, disappointed.

"Golden plover," said Gavin proudly.

"Golden what?"

"They're birds," said Naomi, "that's their name."

"Oh," said Ruth.

Tired and disconsolate, Naomi stumped indoors and up to her bedroom. No treasure at all! Even one small ring, or one single gold coin would have been enough, she reflected. She had not expected to come home completely empty-handed.

"Well, there's still Peter, I suppose," said Ruth coming in, in time to see Naomi push the empty shoe boxes prepared for the loot back under her bed. "I said I'd look after him tomorrow morning while they go to Harvest Festival. And we thought of a way of getting money while you were gone, only it's a bit early in the year. Still, only a few weeks."

"What is it?" asked Naomi suspiciously.

"Well, you know how people do Trick or Treat . . ."

"Oh no!" said Naomi.

"We could dress up Rachel and Phoebe in those old clothes you used for disguises."

"You must be mad!"

"No one would know who they were, all dressed up!"

"They'd know who we were, though!"

"Oh well," said Ruth, "I did wonder if you'd like it. What about carol singing, then?"

"It's not even October yet!"

"The shops have had Christmas cards in for ages," said Ruth earnestly, "and anyway, we thought we needn't do carols straight away, just ordinary hymns, and then get more and more carolly as it gets nearer Christmas . . ."

"It would be terrible," said Naomi bluntly.

Rachel came in and announced that everyone was taking food to the church.

"Cooking apples and tins of beans and all sorts," she said. "Me and Phoebe's been watching them. What happens to it all after Harvest Festival?"

"What happens to church collections?" asked Phoebe, who had followed her in. "That's what I want to know!"

"Look," said Naomi, firmly, "I'll get the next ten pounds. Properly, without robbing the church collection or pinching the Harvest Festival stuff . . ."

"We only wondered about it," Rachel interrupted, "anyway, the church is locked!"

"How do you know?"

"I tried the door. Don't look at me like that! I only wanted to see all the food!"

"Oh yes?" said Naomi sceptically, "and no one's going Trick or Treating or early carol singing either!"

"We didn't *want* to," Ruth said, "I just thought we ought. There's only pocket money and Peter left, and I'm worried about Peter. He's getting too many good habits!"

That was true. Ruth realized it again the next morning. Peter, who had spent the best part of two years scurrying round on his hands and knees with apparently no intention of ever walking upright, was staggering round the Collingwood kitchen.

"He'll soon forget crawling altogether," said Mrs Collingwood complacently. "He's getting to be a proper little man! Milk and biscuits for him on the sideboard, Ruth! See you in an hour or so! Kiss Mummy goodbye!"

Peter not only kissed her goodbye, but hugged Mr Collingwood too, and gravely offered his cheek to Martin. He further alarmed Ruth by waving sedately to his departing family from the window, instead of indulging in his usual practice of going black and screaming.

"Perhaps he's ill," thought Ruth, but not very hopefully, because Peter had never looked better. Or cleaner! It was amazing the difference walking instead of crawling made to his appearance. Gone were the grimy hands and knees and the red, breathless face. Instead he looked pink and white and horribly human. He was even beginning to show a faint resemblance to his brother, who was not called Martin-the-good by his neighbours for nothing. He was, oh horrors, thought Ruth, as she peered closely at his head, beginning to grow hair! Real, shiny hair, hair that looked like it might well be blond and curly, had begun to replace the worn, patchy fluff that had adorned his head for so long. It seemed the final blow. Ruth would have been less distressed to discover he was growing horns.

Naomi, who had been alarmed at her sister's hints about Peter and decided to inspect him for herself, arrived to find Ruth thoughtfully poking his head.

"What are you doing?" she asked. "Has he got fleas or something?"

"Worse," said Ruth. "Look at him! He's growing blond curls! And walking on his back legs and not screaming or smashing things! He's been staring out of the window as good as good, waving to cars!"

"Why's he so clean?" asked Naomi, frowning at Peter's curls. "He must have been up for hours."

"It's because he's stopped crawling."

"Can he talk yet?"

"No. Not really, only Good Dog and bits of Italian and French I've been teaching him. He can't say anything that makes sense."

"Well," said Naomi briskly, "that's not so bad then! First we'll get him crawling again! We'll teach him to play Omelette!"

Omelette was a game played by Ruth and Naomi in their extreme youth. All one needed was a sofa, stout knees in one's clothes and a loud voice. Ruth had not known what an omelette was when she had invented the game; the word alone had fascinated her. It seemed to hold all power and wizardry, and she had crawled round and round the sofa, shouting it at the top of her voice until palms and knees grew hot, and she was dizzy and the world

144

whirled and the word took possession. It was a game that began in excitement, continued into frenzy, and ended in madness and exhaustion. Naomi had learnt it, Mrs Conroy had banned it, and since then, for years, they had forgotten its existence.

Now they looked thoughtfully at Peter, pulled the Collingwoods' beautiful green velvet sofa away from the wall, and began to play again. Peter watched them, startled but fascinated and then flung himself on to the floor to join in.

Never had Omelette been played so ferociously. Ruth and Naomi seemed to have lost the skill of crawling at great speed and dropped out after a few minutes, but Peter continued wildly circling, bellowing his chant of 'OmeletteOmeletteOmelette' until his knees gave way and he collapsed, filthy and red-faced on Naomi's feet.

"Looks more like himself now," said Naomi cheerfully. "What next?"

"Milk and biscuits," said Ruth, suddenly remembering and hurrying off to fetch them.

Peter, hungry from his exercise, gobbled his biscuits as if he were starving and then got very milky down his front attempting to drink by lapping.

"Like Josh," said Naomi, demonstrating.

"Good dog," said Peter, rubbing his milky hands through his curls to dry them, and fell asleep in the corner of the sofa. Ruth, regarding him with pride, reflected that he would need bathing before lunch-time, but then the Peter she had known and loved in the past had always needed scrubbing several times a day.

"Oh my Peter!" exclaimed Mrs Collingwood, on seeing her offspring. "What have you done to poor Ruth!"

"Nothing," said Ruth hastily, "he's been perfectly good! He didn't scream a bit when you left. Naomi came round and we played with him and then he had his milk and biscuits and went to sleep. He's been very good!"

"Well, sweet of you to spare my feelings," said Mrs Collingwood, still staring at Peter. "Soap and hot water I think! Say thank you to Ruth!"

"Grazie good dog," said Peter absently.

"Practically a whole sentence," said Mrs Collingwood, smiling proudly.

"Worked, didn't it?" remarked Naomi complacently when Ruth arrived home. "How much? Got the jam jar, Rachel?"

Rachel fished up the jam jar and dropped the two pound coins Ruth gave her into it.

"If we put in half of everyone's pocket money this week and next week that'll make five. We need another five more."

"Phoebe and I found out train fares to London," said Rachel. "We rang the station and pretended we were taking our grandchildren. We said we were two old ladies!"

"That's what we will be, by the time we get to Africa," said Ruth. "I don't know why you keep talking about it. We don't even know where we'll get another five pounds from!"

"I'll get it," said Naomi.

Joseck and Mari sat together on the schoolhouse steps, waiting to see the bus to Nairobi pass by along the road. Joseck waited because he was fascinated by this bus, and Mari waited because she was not allowed to walk home without Joseck. Not that Mari was in a hurry to get home anyway, she knew quite well that her mother would have errands for her to run, her aunt would be full of questions about the school day, and worst of all, in Mari's opinion, her grandmother would be itching to rearrange Mari's black curls into the intricate patterns that she was famous for. Mari often wished her grandmother had a hundred granddaughters to comb and plait, instead of only one. Every girl in the school envied Mari's beautiful hairdressing, but Mari said it pulled and was bumpy, and spent her days unpicking the knobs, although no sooner would the last twist be free than her grandmother would cry,

"Bring that child to sit by me!" and the whole process would begin again.

"Still here?" The teacher came out of the schoolroom and locked the door.

"Only till the bus comes," said Joseck. "I can see it now, going back to Nairobi and it's not even four o'clock!" and he sighed.

"What's wrong, Joseck?" asked the teacher. "It's a long way back to Nairobi. You know that."

"Yes," agreed Joseck.

"Why worry about the bus?"

"He's worrying about his friends in England," said Mari, busily shaking free her last braid.

The teacher, who was very fond of Joseck, sat down on the step beside him. "Tell me the worry."

"Well," said Joseck slowly, "I know they can't really, but if they *did* come to Africa and *did* catch the bus from Nairobi to visit here, what would happen? The bus passes here at dinner-time and is gone by four o'clock! There would be no time to speak or to go down to the river, or to hear my father's stories. And we have nowhere they could sleep. What would they do?"

The teacher knew all about Joseck's friends in England and he patted Joseck's back reassuringly.

"If your friends ever come, and if they visit us here on the bus from Nairobi and if they are able to stay the night, they will sleep at the schoolhouse!"

"Your house?" asked Joseck, amazed, because the teacher's house was by far the best in the district, wooden and large and shaded by lemon trees.

"My house," agreed the teacher, "but don't hope too

much. I'm afraid your friends dream as much as you do! And, as well, I think they are children and probably not rich."

"Joseck has no sense," Mari remarked, running her fingers with satisfaction through her untidy hair, "and his friends have no sense either! Of course they will not come!"

"And Mari has no sense," said the teacher, surveying her cheerfully as he got to his feet, "because now her grandmother will be after her as soon as she gets home!"

"Perhaps not," said Mari, but she looked very doubtful.

Joseck reported his teacher's invitation in his next letter to England, together with reassurances about goat-consuming snakes.

"Queer to think," said Ruth, "that we have somewhere to stay in Africa!"

"And no snakes to bother about," added Rachel.

"There are snakes, Joseck says."

"Yes, but it was the goat-swallowing ones that were putting me off!"

"Put anyone off," agreed Toby, who had listened with interest to Joseck's letter, "not that I'd want to go, snakes or no snakes!"

"We would, though," said Naomi, "only it's imposs-ible, but if it wasn't, we would!"

Emma, who if she had listened at all to this conver-sation, had listened with her eyes shut, looked up to say, "You lot make problems! Lad's even found you some-where to stay!" and then fell so deeply asleep that even Phoebe could not shake her awake to argue.

"Leave her be," said Toby gently, "she got tired today, sitting out in your garden. Anyway, you'll not talk her round! Leave her be!"

The notice in the shop window read: BOOKS BOUGHT AND SOLD. Naomi paused to reread it before pushing open the door and marching in. She carried two large bags of books, chosen with care, but without permission, from the bookshelves of herself and her sisters.

The shop appeared at first to be empty, but at the thump of Naomi's bags on the floor, a door at the back creaked, and the owner appeared. Naomi was pleased to see that he was thin and bald and looked as nervous as she felt.

"Books bought and sold," she quoted bravely. "I've brought some books."

"To sell?" asked the owner.

"It says that you buy books in the window. What sort of books? Old ones?"

"All sorts. The older the better."

"Some of mine are very old," said Naomi, relieved. "What about children's books?"

"Very collectable these days."

"Well, mine are mostly children's ones," said Naomi, feeling more and more confident, "that me and my sisters have collected."

"And now you want to sell them?"

"That's why I've brought them."

"And your sisters want to sell them too?"

Naomi looked uncomfortable, but reflected that if her sisters did not exactly want to sell them, they certainly wanted the money they would bring.

"We couldn't all come," she said evasively, and began unpacking her bags on to the counter. The first to come out were four Bibles and four prayer books that she had stuffed in at the last minute.

"They *look* new," she said anxiously, watching the bookshop owner pick them up, "but only because we never read them. They're old, really. They were christening presents. You can tell by the dates."

"Ruth, Naomi, Rachel and Phoebe Conroy," read the bookshop owner, studying the dates, "and you are?"

"Naomi. These are really old! That's why the covers have come off."

"Paperbacks."

"Yes, and these are old too."

"School books."

"Not pinched from school," Naomi reassured him. "They were throwing them out last term. These were Mum's, so they're very old!"

"Annuals." The bookshop owner brightened up and began examining the dates, "Any more?"

"These Sunday school prizes that were Grandma's. They look quite new, I'm afraid, but they're really ancient. Only they're full of stories with morals so we never bother with them. Someone might, though."

"Someone might, certainly," agreed the bookshop owner. "Anything more?"

Naomi shook her head and looked anxiously at the pile of books on the counter. "How much will I get?"

"How much were you thinking of?"

"For all of them?"

"Certainly. The annuals and the Sunday school prizes, anyway. I can dispose of the rest if you like."

Naomi sighed with relief and said she wanted as much as possible, preferably twenty-five pounds and the bookshop owner shook his head and said he thought not, and offered five.

"Twenty," said Naomi.

"Sorry, my dear."

"Fifteen?"

"How about ten?" suggested the bookshop owner, "which is as much as you'll get anywhere."

"Ten," said Naomi. "Oh well, ten'll do. Can I have it now?"

"I shall just need your telephone number," the bookshop owner grew suddenly brisk. "Will your mother be at home? Or your father?"

"What for?" asked Naomi, very alarmed to see that the bookshop owner had already pulled a telephone directory from under the counter and was turning up the Conroys.

"Always check with parents before buying off children," he murmured, running his finger down the list. "First rule of business! Good heavens!"

Naomi, horrified, had grabbed her books off the counter, stuffed them back into her bags, yanked open the door and disappeared.

"Good heavens!" repeated the bookshop owner again. "No more than I guessed, though!" and he gazed regretfully for a minute out of the window. It was a pity about the annuals, he thought.

Peter, very black about the knees from playing Omelette, sat in his high chair and ate his egg as beautifully as he had been taught by the Italian waiter. Having finished it, he seized the shell, turned it upside-down and pounded it flat on his tray.

"Good dog?" he asked, looking at his mother out of the corner of his eye.

"Bad dog!" said Mrs Collingwood. "Sorry, darling! I mean Bad Peter! You didn't learn to do that in Italy! Or anywhere else, for that matter! Naughty Peter! Drink your milk!"

"Woof did," remarked Peter, wiping eggshell into his hair.

Mrs Collingwood looked at him in amazement. "I'm sure she didn't, if you said what I think you said!"

"Woof *did*," Peter told himself quietly, reaching for his milk. "Woof did! Woof did!" and he sneezed very hard into his mug.

"*That's* not the way to drink!" said Mrs Collingwood. "Really, Peter! What a mess! You've never done that before!"

Peter looked up with the expression of one determined to see justice done.

"Nayo does!" he said, and bent to try and lap out of his mug again.

"Peter!" exclaimed Mrs Collingwood, just managing to seize it as it tipped.

"Nayo," said Peter firmly, "does!"

Mrs Collingwood said nothing, but looked at him very oddly as she unstrapped him and dumped him on the floor. He dropped to his knees immediately and started playing Omelette round and round the kitchen table.

"Peter," said Mrs Collingwood, "that is a horrid, noisy game. Who plays it with you? Martin? Nursery?"

"Omelette, omelette, omelette!" shouted Peter. "Woof and Nayo play! Woof!"

"Yes," said Mrs Collingwood.

"And Nayo!" said Peter triumphantly.

Chapter Ten

Naomi ran and ran, her breath coming in painful jerks and the heavy bags of books knocking her shins. When she had given in to the impulse to sell their christening presents, she had forgotten all about their names being inside. Now her only hope was to reach home before the bookshop owner could telephone her parents. Perhaps she could answer the phone herself and, disguising her voice, deny all knowledge of Naomi Conroy.

"I always seem to be doing this," reflected Naomi, forcing herself to slow down to a walk, to cross the street beside the church. At the gate the vicar stood, talking to a party of visitors, and Naomi hoped she would not be recognized as the shabby little man who had robbed the street artist only a few weeks before. Strange to see those paving stones bare again! Naomi, walking as quickly and inconspicuously as possible, had a sudden mental image of herself, the dark little man, haunting that spot a hundred years into the future, while Ruth, a shadowy, kneeling ghost, perpetually chalked vanishing pictures on to the pavement.

"Hey Naomi! Wake up!" called a familiar voice, and Naomi looked up to see Gavin grinning down at her from a shining new bike and looking most un-Gavinishly cheerful.

"Nearly ran you over!"

"I'm in an awful rush."

"I'll walk with you a bit. I'd take your bags only my carrier's full already!" Gavin proudly indicated an enormous bulging heap of books, flasks, rugs, binoculars, waterproofs and wellington boots, all strapped in a precarious bundle on to the back of his bike.

"Going bird-watching," he said casually.

Naomi thought it looked more like he was going round the world, and would have said so, if she'd had breath enough to speak.

"Guess how I got the bike," said Gavin.

"Birthday?"

"No. Congratulations present from Dad for dumping Wendy! Anyway, see you!" and he rode off on his bike, before Naomi could begin to reply that it had been obtained under false pretences.

"Wendy dumped him!" she thought, slightly resentfully, as she began to run again, and she thought how strange it was to feel sorry for Wendy. Funny how much nicer she had become since she went in for women's lib!

"Wish I was liberated!" thought Naomi, and tried to imagine a life free from old people who needed gardens, African boys who needed educating and useless sisters who needed locking up.

Above her head the church clock struck three. How long had it been since she left the bookshop, she wondered? More than five minutes? Time to have found her telephone number yet? Nothing to do but carry on running, while all the time her hands grew more sore and numb from the bumping bags of books.

Nearly home, anyway. Naomi slowed down again and swopped the bags over. Past Rachel and Phoebe's school, and the Thin One's house, where the Thin One was actually swinging on the gate. He peered eagerly into Naomi's bags as she passed and asked, "Where's Rachel and Phobe?"

"Home, eating enormous sandwiches," replied Naomi cruelly, and hurried on.

"Wait for me!"

Naomi turned crossly and saw that the Thin One had left his gate and was running after her.

"Can I come home with you?"

"No you can't! What for?"

"A sandwich?" said the Thin One hopefully.

"No you definitely can't! Go home!"

To shake him off, Naomi dashed into the Post Office and then dashed out again as the counter staff all burst into laughter and threw their hands up in the air. The Thin One, disconsolate, stood in the doorway and watched her all down the road.

Two minutes later Naomi, tottering with exhaustion, jogged slowly past the Collingwoods' house, looked thankfully along to her own, and came to a sudden, dismayed halt.

Something was happening. Mrs Collingwood was in the front garden, talking earnestly to Ruth, who was looking most uncomfortable. Their mother was listening with a very grim expression on her face. From the Conroys' open front door came the sudden sound of the telephone ringing, and Mrs Conroy disappeared inside to answer it.

"Nayo!" cried Peter, suddenly catching sight of his friend and bouncing with delight. Naomi, after one startled glance, instinctively turned and fled, pursued by cries of "Nayo! Nayo! Nayo!" faint and plaintive, hunting her through the streets.

Confused and horrible thoughts pounded through Naomi's head as she struggled along. The bookshop owner had found her number and telephoned her mother, and she had been seen, caught red-handed with her arms full of evidence. No chance of slipping in quietly now. Ruth was in trouble, that was clear, and Peter had learned to talk! It was impossible not to imagine that the facts were unconnected. What on earth should she do with these horrible books? And, for that matter, what on earth should she do with herself?

All at once, the solution came to her. She would go to Toby and Emma's and leave the books in their garden shed, and then she would go to the house and sit in their quiet, bare room and do nothing. Rest. Not even think. And Toby and Emma, with whom no secrets were necessary, would let her.

With the exhausted, peaceful feeling of waking from a nightmare, Naomi wandered through the streets to Toby and Emma's bungalow.

"We ought to cut the grass," she said to herself as she came within sight of it. The lawn was beginning to look ragged and shaggy, scattered with fallen yellow leaves. Autumn had arrived in the garden. The borders, although still bright with flowers, had a tumbled, dishevelled appearance. Recent winds had brought small, yellow apples down from the apple tree and they littered the ground and path, scabby and unappetizing.

"I'll pick them up before I go in," decided Naomi, pleased to think of one useful thing she could accomplish that afternoon. It was strange not to find Emma in the garden. Lately, she had spent every bright afternoon nodding by the flower-beds, tucked up in layers of rugs and blankets against the chilly wind.

Naomi glanced across at the windows to see if anyone was looking out. Nobody was there, but the front door opened and Mrs Reed appeared. It was only then that Naomi noticed the cars parked outside the house.

"Have they got visitors?" she asked Mrs Reed, surprised.

Mrs Reed, catching sight of Naomi for the first time, stared at her in concern. "Yes, visitors," she agreed after a moment. "Shouldn't you be at home?"

"Why?" asked Naomi. "It's Saturday! We always come and see them at the week-end but if they've got people there, I'll just leave these bags in the shed."

Mrs Reed, however, appeared to think otherwise, and with a hand on Naomi's back, she steered her away from Toby and Emma's gate. Naomi tried to wriggle away, but Mrs Reed, a headmistress, was an expert at steering unwilling people. Over the years, with that firm hand between the shoulders, she had steered hundreds of reluctant people in directions they did not wish to take: sinners to people's desks to confess, the unwashed to cloakrooms, heroes and heroines on to public stages to receive prizes, sworn enemies to face-to-face confrontations with each other, where they were forced to shake hands and say sorry. Now she steered Naomi to her car, opened the door, took possession of the bags of books and stowed them, together with her outraged and ungrateful passenger, into the front seat.

"I'll drop you off at home," she said. "I need to see your mother."

'Another person complaining,' thought Naomi, alarmed, and glanced at Mrs Reed apprehensively. She did not look angry; tired and worried, perhaps, but kindly.

"I don't want to go home yet," Naomi told her. "I really wanted to leave these things in the shed. I could have easily waited there until their visitors were gone. I wanted to get the apples picked up, anyway; they've fallen all over the path. Couldn't you just drop me off?"

Mrs Reed did not answer for a minute, and when she did all she would say was, "Don't worry about the apples, Naomi."

Naomi, subsiding sulkily into her seat, wondered what awaited her at home. As the car pulled up outside the Conroys' gate, she was relieved to see that there was no one in the garden. Mrs Collingwood and Peter had disappeared, but Ruth stood at their bedroom window, staring out into the street, looking unhappy and mutinous. She jumped as she saw Mrs Reed and Naomi climb out of the car, and then, as Mrs Reed hurried ahead to the front door, she caught Naomi's eye, pointed firmly at herself and then her sister, and drew a horizontal line across her throat with her finger.

'Both of us in trouble, then,' thought Naomi, as she sidled to the front door behind Mrs Reed.

"Mrs Reed!" exclaimed Naomi's mother, answering the front door, and then, catching sight of her daughter skulking in the background, "Naomi!" in a tone that bode no good at all for Naomi. She got no further, however. Mrs Reed laid a gentle hand on Mrs Conroy's arm, shook her head slightly and asked if she might have a quick word. Naomi seized the opportunity to escape upstairs to Ruth.

"You got away quickly!" said Ruth, as she opened the door. "Mum's planning to kill you, when she's done me! What did Mrs Reed want? Are Rachel and Phoebe in trouble now? S'pose you realize Peter's learnt to talk?"

Naomi dropped the bags of books with a sigh of relief. "Feels like I've been carrying them for years," she remarked, kicking them under her bed (where they remained for the next six months). "I don't know the answers to any of your questions," and she flopped down wearily on to the quilt.

"A man from a bookshop rang up about you!" Rachel and Phoebe burst into the room. "What's Mrs Reed doing here?"

"She's probably come about you," said Ruth. "What have you done?"

"Nothing at all," said Phoebe.

"Lately," said Rachel, "I don't think. It's getting hard to remember everything people say we've done wrong. Do you want to know what the man from the bookshop said about you?"

"No." Naomi rolled over on to her back and closed her eyes.

"Well, don't you want to know what Peter went and said?"

"No. I don't care. I've given up caring!"

"What about?"

"Everything," said Naomi dreamily. "It's a lovely feeling!"

Ruth, Rachel and Phoebe stared at her crossly. They had no intention of leaving her to wallow in lovely, non-caring feelings while they suffered with their consciences.

"The man from the bookshop said you were trying to sell books that didn't seem to belong to you!"

"They didn't," agreed Naomi placidly, "so he was right. They were mostly yours, actually."

"And he said you ran off very guiltily. He hoped you got home all right. Mum said she'd send you round to apologize for wasting his time."

"She won't."

"She's furious!"

"Poor Mum," said Naomi, still with her eyes shut.

"And Peter's told Mrs Collingwood we taught him to play Omelette. And that I showed him how to bash up his eggshells and you showed him how to lap up milk, like a dog. And Mrs Collingwood said she wasn't angry . . ."

"Well then," said Naomi, "what's it matter?"

"But very puzzled. And Mum said we weren't to be trusted."

"Well, I s'pose she's right," agreed Naomi.

"Don't you care what happens to us?"

"No."

"Don't you know why Mrs Reed is here?" asked Rachel, who had been very quiet, trying to work out which of her many recent sins might have come to her headmistress's attention. "I don't suppose you care about that, either!"

"Not a bit," agreed Naomi, cheerfully.

"How are we going to get Joseck's money? Or don't you care?"

"I don't know. Someone else will have to think of something. I've run out of ideas."

"Where did Mrs Reed grab you?"

"Toby and Emma's."

"I thought we might go tomorrow," said Ruth. "Are they all right?"

Naomi opened her eyes and sat up, suddenly remembering something she did still care about.

"I don't know. I didn't see them. Mrs Reed grabbed me at the gate and I couldn't get away. There were cars outside and she said they had visitors."

"They couldn't have," said Phoebe, "they never do. Emma says she can't be bothered with people who treat her like she's old . . ."

At that moment the bedroom door was pushed open and Mrs Reed came in, followed by Mrs Conroy.

"Treat who like she's old?" asked Mrs Reed, sitting down on Naomi's bed.

"Emma." Phoebe stared at her headmistress in astonishment. "But we never do. Why?"

"I just wondered who you were talking about," said Mrs Reed, "I'm sure you never did. That's why she loved having you there so much."

Startled by something they could not name, Ruth and Naomi glanced at each other and then at their mother. For the first time they noticed her eyes.

"Emma died this morning," said Mrs Conroy, and all the jigsaw puzzle pieces of Naomi's afternoon fell slowly into place.

Chapter Eleven

The Conroy girls were in disgrace. They had been in it for a week and so far there seemed to be no possibility of them ever being in any other state. It was not the familiar, shabby state of disgrace in which one or another of them had spent so much of the spring and summer, and from which they might expect to drift out, forgotten, forgiven and reinstated into family life. This was bad, awful, dire disgrace. Their mother was ashamed of them. She felt she could not ignore or help or understand her daughters. She treated them with furious bewilderment.

This had been going on since she and Mrs Reed waited anxiously in Ruth and Naomi's bedroom for the reaction to the news of Emma's death.

"Emma dead?" exclaimed Ruth in dismay. "That's all we need!" And Naomi horrified her mother still further by pulling her pillow over her head and announcing that she did not care.

"I don't care," repeated Naomi, "I don't care, I don't care. I've stopped caring about everything!"

Phoebe waited until the room was quiet and then announced cheerfully, "It's not true and I don't believe it!"

No amount of explanations had been able to convince her. The only tears shed that afternoon had been by Rachel; and she, on closer inspection, was found to be crying over a jam jar of money.

"Things will get better." Mr Conroy repeated this hope over and over again to his wife as the week progressed, but as far as Mrs Conroy could see, things only got worse.

"Look," said Ruth on Saturday night, "we're not doing any good howling like this. We ought to go straight down to poor old Toby's. It's too late now, but we could go tomorrow."

On Sunday, however, Mrs Conroy flatly refused to let them out of the house. Ruth and Naomi had not argued, but the next morning they did not catch the school bus.

"If there's someone there, we'll come away," said Naomi, "or if he looks like he wants to be on his own."

But there was no one else there, and Toby, who seemed to have been expecting them, showed no signs of wanting to be alone.

"Tell us when you want us to go," said Ruth. "We thought you might be lonely."

"What about school?" asked Toby.

"Blow school," said Naomi briefly.

"Ay well, it does get like that sometimes," Toby agreed, and said no more on the subject. He seemed so pleased to have someone to talk to, that Ruth and Naomi stayed until their usual time for leaving school, returned home, and repeated the performance for the next two days.

"I wish Phoebe and me could come too," said Rachel, "but Mrs Reed would notice and Mum would get even crosser. Phoebe's in awful trouble now, too."

Phoebe, after having totally ignored the subject for two days, had marched up to Naomi on Monday night and demanded, "Is Emma really dead?"

"You know she is," Naomi told her, and Phoebe had not replied, but later on that night Mrs Conroy had noticed a change in Phoebe's zoo. The inmates who had languished there for so many months had all been released. Instead, every cage was littered with slips of paper. Emma's name was on all of them.

"Why, Phoebe?" Mrs Conroy had asked.

"Because she is dead," said Phoebe, furious, but unable to find the words to explain that as far as she was concerned

Emma had deserted her, left her friend to cope alone, vanished in the middle of an argument, died without a word of explanation or farewell.

Phoebe, with no intention of letting her escape so easily, put her in the zoo, and Mrs Conroy found her there and threw all the cages away and cried. Phoebe did not cry. She went to her father, who asked,

"What can I do to help you, Phoebe?"

"Give me five pounds," said Phoebe, suddenly remembering something that really would help.

It was not the answer her father had expected, and instead of giving her five pounds he rather angrily sent her to bed. Phoebe stamped upstairs, converted her slipper into a temporary cage and put him in it.

"I wish their grandmother was here," said Mr Conroy. "She might make more sense of them than I can."

Mrs Conroy said it was just plain naughtiness on Phoebe's part, but when on Tuesday night, Rachel appeared in her parents' bedroom, tear-stained and miserable, and asking not for comfort, as Mrs Conroy had hoped, but for an advance on their pocket money, she began to think otherwise. On Wednesday, when a phone call revealed that Ruth and Naomi had not attended school all week, she rang Big Grandma and asked for help.

When Ruth, Naomi, Rachel and Phoebe came home from Toby's on Friday night, an astonishing sight met their eyes. Hands on hips, gazing sternly down the road at them, stood a battered old lady.

"Big Grandma!" they shrieked, and broke into a run.

"Big Grandma indeed!" snapped Big Grandma, as they reached her. "I think you people have some explaining to do!"

"Oh Big Grandma!" Rachel hugged her round her iron waist.

"Why did you come?" asked Ruth.

"To save your poor mother from madness," replied Big Grandma. "Go on Phoebe! Ask me! I'm waiting! How much?"

"Five pounds, please," replied Phoebe meekly.

Silently Big Grandma handed her the money, Rachel plunged her hand down her front and extracted a jam jar of coins, Naomi dashed inside and returned with an envelope, and Ruth, seizing jam jar, envelope and five pound note, sprinted away round the corner to the Post Office. She returned a few minutes later, out of breath but smiling with relief.

"Happy now?" asked Big Grandma sarcastically, "or just happy until November? What do you plan to do then?"

"Naomi's birthday's in November," said Rachel, "birthday money."

"Out of interest," said Big Grandma, "what would you have done had I not turned up this evening and bailed you out?"

"Trick or Treat, or early carol singing," said Phoebe.

"No we wouldn't," said Naomi.

"We could have done sledge rides, I thought," said Rachel, "only there isn't any snow."

"I wondered about duck food for the ducks in the park," said Ruth, "selling it to people to feed to them. But we didn't really think it would be much good."

"Not enough ducks," explained Rachel, "and all very fat."

"I must say," remarked Big Grandma, "it's obviously a very good job I came when I did! However, put it all behind you! There's a reception committee waiting inside to cross-question you."

"Who?"

"Your mother, as chief (and most indignant) sufferer, your father, home early from work on purpose, Mrs Collingwood in the dual capacity of Emma's solicitor and unwilling victim of your ingenuity, one of many I might add, and myself as interested bystander!"

"Now what have we done?" demanded Naomi.

"You may well ask," said Big Grandma.

"I haven't done anything wrong for ages," said Rachel.

"No, neither have I," protested Phoebe, as she was propelled in to the reception committee. "There's nothing wrong with putting people in zoos when they tell you that everything's easy and then go and die, without helping."

"My poor sausage!" said Mrs Collingwood, hearing this remark and catching sight of Phoebe's unhappy face. "My poor sausage, come here!"

Rachel, who had rushed upstairs for her sledge, stamped sulkily into the room, holding it like a battering ram and remarked, "No one calls me a poor sausage, and I haven't done anything wrong, except what other people made me do and I did to be kind, and now I'm in trouble! I don't think it's fair!" She positioned her sledge like a wall and got down behind it.

"Nobody is in trouble," Mrs Conroy said. "Well, that's not true. I'm very angry with all of you. You've all been very silly. Why ever didn't you tell us about this boy in Africa?"

"How do you know about him?" Ruth and Naomi spoke together.

"Your grandmother seems to have gathered what you were up to," replied Mrs Conroy, "and anyway, Emma told Mrs Collingwood."

"Emma told?" asked Phoebe furiously. "Good job she's dead then, I say!"

"Phoebe!" exclaimed Mrs Conroy, and then, seeing the tears running down Phoebe's face, put an arm round her.

"She said we were friends," sobbed Phoebe, "the sneaking pig! And I gave her a zoo and everything!"

"Oh well," said Ruth bravely, "it was all my fault. We

couldn't tell you because he was illegal, because I put that I was eighteen instead of thirteen. And anyway, when I talked to you about it ages ago, you said you didn't believe in it."

"Illegal?" asked Mrs Conroy. "Because you said you were eighteen? What about all the other illegal things you've done, since?"

"Only robbing the Post Office once," said Rachel sulkily, "and it was my own money!"

"And selling sandwiches made in a dog kennel," said Mrs Conroy, "and being street artists, for goodness sake! And you should never have taken those books Naomi, and you knew it! And poor Mrs Collingwood, Ruth! It may not be illegal, teaching babies bad habits, but it certainly isn't very responsible!"

"I didn't want him to grow up too quick," said Ruth, "so that he wouldn't need me to look after him anymore, because I needed the money for Joseck."

"Emma had to tell me," explained Mrs Collingwood, "because I was her solicitor . . ."

"And because she's a horrible . . ."

"Hang on, Phoebe," said Mrs Collingwood, "because I was her solicitor and she wanted to give some money to your friend in Africa . . ."

"Emma hadn't got any money," said Ruth. "Neither has Toby. They're as poor as poor, you should see their house. We had to stop charging them for the gardening in the end."

"It was because you didn't charge them for the gardening that Emma asked to see me," continued Mrs Collingwood patiently, "and because you'd been their friends and given Emma such a lovely summer, and they knew you needed money. Emma and Toby have, had I should say, although Toby still has of course, quite a lot of money," said Mrs Collingwood. "They sold a large farm, you know. They were rather lonely, it made a lot of difference you being there and making such friends with them. You stopped them feeling so old."

"Being old isn't any excuse for anything," said Phoebe, "especially sneaking!"

"Emma asked to see me," Mrs Collingwood continued, "and I helped her make a new will, where she left enough money to see Joseck through his school years and to start him off a little afterwards, because she said she owed you that much for the summer in the garden, and she also left a little bit of money for you girls, not a lot, she said to tell you, in case you got soft! Enough, she said, to get you to Africa, and a little bit over to get you back!"

"But that was just a little joke," said Mrs Conroy hastily, "she would know you couldn't really go. It's yours anyway, to put in the bank for when you leave school."

"Enough for Joseck to stay at school?" asked Naomi, flabbergasted, "and for us to go to Africa?"

"Is it true?" asked Phoebe. "Is that why she sneaked?"

"Yes, it's true and that's why she sneaked," Mrs Collingwood told her, "so don't cry, Phoebe, she didn't stop being your friend. That was her way of helping you."

But nothing could stop Phoebe crying and the tears were catching. Even Big Grandma snorted rather damply. Mrs Collingwood went home and the meeting broke up in disarray.

The first thing Rachel said when she awoke was, "It's a good job about those snakes!"

There was no reply from the bottom bunk because Phoebe was in the dining room, helping Ruth and Naomi write to Joseck.

"It's a good job about those snakes!" she said to her sisters in greeting, and they agreed that it was.

"What are you telling Joseck?"

"About the money and about us coming. Mrs Collingwood's writing to him too, but we thought we would as well."

"Tell him I'm sorry about my sledge."

"What about it?"

"I'm sure I won't be able to take it," explained Rachel gravely. "Mum wouldn't even let me take it to Big Grandma's in the summer!"

"We're trying to keep this letter simple," said Naomi. "It's hard enough to tell him everything anyway, without having to write a load of rubbish about your sledge!"

"You can say you're sorry about your sledge when you get there, if you like," said Ruth. "This letter is finished unless you have anything sensible to tell him that won't take much space."

"Say it's a good job about the snakes, then."

Rachel says, wrote Ruth,

   it is a good job about those snakes.
Love from Ruth, Naomi, Rachel and Phoebe.

"You people are up early!" Big Grandma came into the dining room to find her granddaughters, all in various states of undress, sealing up Joseck's envelope. "Is that a letter for Africa? I can take it, if you like, I was going to the letter-box myself. Go and get dressed, I'll be back before you're down to breakfast. May I have a look at Joseck's letters, do you think?"

"I'll fetch them down," said Ruth.

Big Grandma smiled to herself as she walked along the road to the letter-box, and then glancing at Ruth's envelope she noticed the address for the first time and paused, startled.

"We'll need passports," said Rachel at breakfast time. "You get the forms from the Post Office. I asked Martin. Bags not me get them!"

"No good going at the hottest time of the year," Big Grandma remarked. "You'd be too exhausted to enjoy it."

"Don't encourage them," said Mrs Conroy. "That was just Emma's little joke, fares to Africa. She wouldn't have expected them to go for one minute!"

"Emma'd be furious if we didn't go, when it was all sorted out," said Ruth.

"Well, it's not all sorted out."

"We've written and told Joseck we're coming," Naomi's voice sounded slightly triumphant, "so we'll have to go now!"

"We've got somewhere to stay," said Rachel, "and it's all right about those snakes. Pity about my sledge, though!"

"What *are* you talking about?" asked her mother. "How do you think four children are going to get to the middle of nowhere in Africa, for goodness sake?"

"Train to London," said Phoebe.

"Half fare," put in Rachel.

"Fly to Nairobi," Ruth said, "we found out the prices ages ago. You have to book in advance, though, but I expect there's plenty of time."

"Bus out to Joseck's school," finished Naomi. "There's one every day, and the teacher said we could stop at the schoolhouse. Joseck asked him and he offered."

"In a minute," said Mrs Conroy, "I shall get very cross!"

"Well, we've posted the letter to say we're coming now," said Naomi, "Big Grandma took it. Did you post it?"

"Certainly," replied Big Grandma cheerfully.

"Really, Mother!" exclaimed Mrs Conroy. "That money is going in the bank! Emma was a very old lady and perhaps didn't understand things very clearly anymore . . ."

"Imagine," said Rachel, "when I die and go to heaven and see Emma and she says, 'Did you like Africa?' and I say, 'I didn't go, none of us did,' and she says, 'What did you spend my money on, then?' and I say, 'Mum made us put it in the bank!' Emma would go mad! Anyway, I'm never putting money in the bank again. It's too hard to get back out!"

"Anyway," added Phoebe, "Emma's not going to heaven! She told me! She's going to haunt places. We worked out loads of good places we'd haunt, we used to choose them in the shed. I'm going to do it too, as soon as I'm dead!"

"I don't know why I'm sitting here listening to this nonsense," exclaimed Mrs Conroy. "The money is going in the bank!"

"Morning!" Mr Conroy came in at that moment. "Hope you realize you'll have to leave that sledge behind, Rachel!"

"John!" exclaimed his wife.

"Will you look after it for me?" asked Rachel.

"I'm not promising to take it to bed every night, if that's what you mean!"

"John!" interrupted Mrs Conroy. "Don't you start! You know quite well they can't possibly go. There's no one free to take them, for one thing!"

"I could take them," said Big Grandma.

There was a silence while this idea sank in and then Rachel said, "Yes, she could take us! She hasn't got a job or anything important to do!"

"Thank you, Rachel!" said Big Grandma.

"Are you really volunteering?" Mr Conroy asked Big Grandma. "It's more than good of you, but . . ."

"It's a part of the world I've thought about a good deal recently," Big Grandma said, "and this morning I discovered something very strange. It seems I've been sponsoring a child in the same school as young Joseck . . ."

The girls stared at her in complete astonishment.

"Is that how you guessed so much?" asked Naomi. "You guessed in the summer, didn't you?"

"More or less," agreed Big Grandma, "and when you

showed me Joseck's letters this morning and I read about Mari . . ."

"Are you Mari's lady?" demanded Ruth.

"I suppose I am," said Big Grandma, "and although I realize their particular school must have been targeted for help this year, still, it seemed so odd, it startled me . . . It seemed like Fate," said Big Grandma.

Chapter Twelve

When everything was finally explained to him, Joseck could hardly believe his good fortune. To have enough money to go to school for as long as he liked was marvellous enough but,

"One day you might go to the university in Nairobi," said his teacher.

"Is there enough for that?"

"Plenty for that. You could train to be a doctor or a scientist or anything. You might travel all over the world!"

"I would go to England," said Joseck, "to see my friends! But first they are coming here!"

"Only because my lady is bringing them!" said Mari. She did not envy Joseck his chance of education at all, but she did, very much, envy Ruth, Naomi, Rachel and Phoebe their grandmother. She and Joseck had pored over the photograph of the girls until it was almost worn away and Mari had formed a private plan to take them to visit her grandmother.

"Because, look at their hair!" she said. "What a mess! They are so lucky; *their* grandmother must never plait it or twist it or even comb it!" There was enough hairdressing on the heads of Joseck's friends, Mari decided, to satisfy *her* grandmother for a very long time.

"When are they coming?" she asked Joseck.

It was a long time before all the plans could be arranged in England. There was a great deal to be decided, even after Mrs Conroy had been persuaded to let them go, but finally there came a day when Martin-the-good could saunter to the bus stop and climb straight on the school bus and sit down. It felt very strange.

The bus continued to wait until Wendy asked, "Why aren't we going?"

They had a new driver that morning, and he seemed in a very bad temper as he replied,

"Chap who usually does this run told me not to pull off without picking up two girls at this stop. Always late, he said."

"Where is the old driver?" asked Wendy nosily.

"Off on his holidays! Won the pools! Nice for some. Where's those two girls, then?"

"Gone to Africa," said Martin.

"Africa!" said the driver. "Where next!"

Africa.

For the last time on the long journey from Nairobi the bus slowed down and stopped.

"This is where we wrote our letters to," said Ruth.

"Yes."

"Out you get," ordered Big Grandma.

Rather stiff and wobbly after the ride, the girls climbed down and looked about themselves. There were blue hills on the horizon and there was a river with green trees, and a wooden schoolhouse. For a moment it seemed as if there was no one about, and then the door of the school opened and a boy, thin and smiling and dressed in white, came shyly out.

"Let them say hello to Joseck first," the teacher cautioned his seething class, but Mari, catching sight of the person who had followed the four girls out of the bus, shot past him, out of the door, and ignoring Joseck and his friends, hurled herself on the old lady who was waiting in the background.

"Hello, Big Grandma!" said Mari.

THE EXILES

Hilary McKay

Winner of the Guardian Children's Fiction Prize

Shock! Horror! The four Conroy sisters are being bundled off to spend the summer holidays with Big Grandma!

Big Grandma makes the girls go for walks in the pouring rain. Worse still, she expects them to do chores – lots of chores – and won't let them have any books to read.

But no one, not even Big Grandma, can stop the Conroy sisters from having fun, from bucket-fishing to bone-collecting, and wreaking havoc along the way.

THE EXILES IN LOVE

Hilary McKay

Love strikes the Conroy sisters – Ruth first.

The school bus-driver captures her heart, but before long she's pining for Jane Eyre's Mr Rochester, too. Then there's the school dreamboat, Alan Adair. Not to mention Mr Blyton Jones, the temporary English teacher, who even catches Naomi's eye.

As if that weren't enough, Big Grandma arranges for Philippe from France to visit. Nobody, not even Phoebe, remains immune to his charms for long . . .